MW01612858

Time Wars

by

Randall Miller

PITTSBURGH, PENNSYLVANIA 15222

The contents of this work including, but not limited to, the accuracy of events, people, and places depicted; opinions expressed; permission to use previously published materials included; and any advice given or actions advocated are solely the responsibility of the author, who assumes all liability for said work and indemnifies the publisher against any claims stemming from publication of the work.

All Rights Reserved
Copyright © 2013 by Randall Miller

No part of this book may be reproduced or transmitted, downloaded, distributed, reverse engineered, or stored in or introduced into any information storage and retrieval system, in any form or by any means, including photocopying and recording, whether electronic or mechanical, now known or hereinafter invented without permission in writing from the publisher.

RoseDog Books
701 Smithfield Street
Pittsburgh, PA 15222
Visit our website at *www.rosedogbookstore.com*

ISBN: 978-1-4349-3487-1
eISBN: 978-1-4349-3365-2

Epitaph-14th century via French epitaphe from ultimately Greek epitaphion
"something above a tomb or burial" from taphos "funeral ceremonies, tomb"

On brightest days or darkest nights, in rain or snow, Epitaph cometh.

On desert dunes or swelling seas, with calming breezes or blustering winds. It matters not for Epitaph will cometh.

His armies care not for men, women, or childern, all they see is trampled into the ground, for Epitaph commands it.

Flying ships, diving monsters, giant wagons pulled by nothing, all spit fire and lightning and make the earth a wasteland, all for the bringer of destruction, Epitaph.

So never sleep or rest in peace, turn laughter into tears, you never know for there is no warning when Epitaph appears.

I wish I could claim this as a Randall Miller original but unfortunately I can't. It's a toast known as The Lafayette Escadrille song sung, I believe by U.S. airmen stationed in France during World War One. However I thought it too be so cool and it fits this story so very well that I just had to include it.

We meet beneath the surrounding rafters, the walls all aroud us are bare. They echo with peels of laughter, seems that the dead are there.

So stand by, your glasses steady, the world is a web of lies. Here's a toast to the dead already, hurrah to the next man who dies.

The author would like to thank the following individuals.

The entire 2010 Cosmos crew for putting up with me all year long. THANK YOU CARLEY for being a friend when I needed one.

Donna Reiser- for treating me as her own kid

Erich Reiser - your just so damn funny

The blond haired girl at the Putnum County Library (Where a lot of this was researched at) for not smacking this weirdo up along side the head. I never did get your name so I just call you "my library friend"

Special thank you's to the following:

John Anderson - acting creative consultant

Matt (Porkchop) Ellis - all necessary computer work

Extra Special Thanks goes out to Nancy Barbaria for motivating my lazy-ass to get this done (sorry it took so long)

Also would like to thank all my friends who over the years have continued to have faith and believe in me even when I FAILED to believe in myself. You all know who you are. THANKS GUYS

Time Wars

By Randall Miller

INTRODUCTION

Hello and many greetings too you the reader. Before we go any further I just thought that you the reader should know that this IS a story of time travel and time manipulation. You will be wisked away to times, lands, and eras long since past. Experience the raw, brutal, barbaric violence that one time ran rampant across and through-out the entire world. Follow me in my travels and journeys for my lord and master, Epitaph.

I must say that even though I do not know the true name of The Epitaph, I do know that he comes from the late twentieth or early twenty-first century. Standing at six feet, seven inches tall and weighing two hundred fifty to three hundred pounds, he is normal stature for that era. I should know, for I have visited that era on occasion. Ah, the sights, pleasures and luxuries of that time. The cities with their tall skyscraper buildings. I never knew men could constuct such wonders. Some are even taller than The Roman Coliseum or The Lighthouse of Alexandria. This is no small feet for the colosseum itself is about one hundred and sixty feet tall, betwixt five hundred and five hundred fifteen feet wide and around six hundred twenty feet long. This archaic edifice was constructed between the years seventy and eighty A.D. by the Roman Emporer Vespasian. Originally called The Flavian Ampitheater, it was financed by the plunder of Jerusalem when it was conquered after a long siege in seventy A.D. With a seating capacity of forty too eighty thousand, it was able too swiftly rush the people in and out of it's eighty entrances within minutes. Now do not think that the people suffered under the hot, blistering sun. No, not by far, for their was one hundred and ten drinking fountains and two very large lavatories. Their was also a twenty-four ton cloth called a velarium that acted as a primitive, retractable roof. This retractable roof, or velarium was supported by two hundred and forty brackets. Each bracket had a tall beam of wood with a system of ropes and pulleys that was worked by about three hundred men. Some say they were sailors but more than likely they were slaves.

Now thats not forget about the two level sub-structure that was hidden and obscured by the wooden, sand covered, arena floor. Beneath and disguised by the floor of the arena were many corridors and passageways, almost like a labyrinth. Amidst this twisting, turning, meandering labyrinth was thirty-two elevators and many trap doors that lifted both elaborate, intricate, recreated scenery and exotic animals from all over the Roman Empire to the surface of the arena floor.

Now even though I was not present for the grand, spectacular opening in eighty A.D., which was celebrated with one hundred days of fervor, bloodshed, and violence. I did just so happen too be there the day that as two buff, well toned, muscular gladiators were squaring off in the circular arena. Viciously and furiously attacking one another. Which from where I was, high up in the stands, not only could you not hear the clashing and clanging of their swords and shields striking one another, but you could barely see the combatants themselves. Not because of the distance, but because of all the sand they (the combatants) would kick up while parrying with one another. But this all came too a sudden halt when one lone, renegade individual, for some unknown reason decided too jump into the arena and put a stop too the fight. I may admire his valiant effort too stop the chaotic madness, however, unfortunately, for him the Romans did not see it this way. You must understand that this would be the equivalent of someone jumping out of the crowd and running across the field of play of the N.F.L. superbowl. The fans would not be happy, and neither were the Romans. In fact they were so upset and enraged that they literally stoned this poor man too death. That may seem a little harsh or out of line but that was a fitting punishment for those times.

Ah. The Lighthouse of Alexandria. The place of so many fond childhood memories for me. Much time I spent walking the shore of Alexandria, gazing at this four hundred foot, mesmerizing wonder. It's white, marble surface, reflecting off the Mediterranean Sea under the stary moonlight. The waves of the water violently crashing off of this constructed superstructure, which at one time was the tallest building in the world outside of The Pyramid of Giza. Sometimes I would have a few of my servants row me out to The Island of Pharos itself, which is where the lighthouse actually stood, in the Harbor of Alexandria. However usually I would just stroll along the beach, bathing in the light of the intense flame that emanated from the lighthouse top too pierce the blackened night sky as well as welcome any and all wayward ships. Either night or day, the beam of the lighthouse could be seen thirty-five miles away. Though it was a fire that gave off the light at night, it was the suns own rays by day, reflected off of finely polished sheets of bronze and cooper. At the very top of this magnificent building was a golden statue of the greek god Poseidon. Believe me, if you were too stand before this spectacle you would stand in awe. It's sheer size alone would take your breath away.

Our escapade begins in The Mediterranean Sea because of The Epitaph babbling something about needing a control experiment. It's because of that reason alone as too why The Epitaph himself actually came with us on this mission, which is in itself a rarity. He wanted too witness first hand as too how this would go over. How this initial intrusion back into time is a control experiment is beyond me. We went back already knowing that even though on this particular mission we would be doing everything we could too blend in with the inhabitants of this time era, all other intrusions in time too follow would be carried out with us being armed and equipped with what you would call modern technology and what the people of history would call the weapons of god or the work of the devil. Anyhow, back too our story. We spent months building ships, forging weapons, making primitive and ancient armor, etc... after all, we were about to try and blend into twelve hundred B.C., or should I say we did. Rather successfully I will add. We looted, pillaged, killed, destroyed, burnt whole villages, slaughtered live-stock, whatever you can imagine, we did it, but my personal favorite is that we left entire empires lying in ashes and ruins. Empires such as the Mycenaeans, Minoans, Hittites, and Canaanites. Our first raids were comparable to a overgrown schoolyard bully picking on the smallest, skinniest kid there. It was simply no contest.

Our first victims were the people of Crete. We savagely charged the island with our swords wildly flailing above our heads. Belligerently yelling and screaming as loudly as humanly possible. Dressed in our light, leather armour with our leather helmets and wooden, cowhide covered shields, we would row our boats in close enough to land, while shooting arrows at the fleeing residence, who were mainly shepherds, farmers, and fishermen. Then we would jump out into about three and a half too four feet of water and wade to shore. Though the pressure of the water around your legs would hinder and slow your progress, the rough waves going into shore would actually push you into the land. Once there, the brutal fun would begin. Our bronze age swords drawn, we would give chase too the fleeing natives, who by now had put quite a bit of distance between us and them. We would dash over the dead and dying. Literally stepping on the bodies in our mad pursuit of our human prey. Stopping only too chop off a finger for a ring, cut off a head for a necklace, or too put some suffering soul out of their misery. We ran down and brutally murdered as many as possible, however most actually made it to the high, rough, steep mountains, and once they were there, they were as safe as a church. We would not pursue them into the steep, arduous mountains. Not only were they thousands of feet above sea-level, but the trails into these mountains hugged the cliff sides, therefore we would have too drop our shields and sheath our swords to climb these barely wide enough for one person paths that not only could be easily defended by the native inhabitants, but a unsure step and one would surely plummet to their death. We raided Crete about a hundred times or so. Using the same methods over and over again. The archers shooting their arrows as we row into land, then our foot soldiers would charge. Tens of thousands of them. Swarming ashore like locust. To the people of Crete as well as arcaeologists these raids lasted years, maybe even decades. To us however, because of Epitaph's time machine, which i'll discuss later, these raids took only mere days. As for the rest of the Mediterranean, that did take us months. Being that Crete is a island and it's natives quickly took to the hills word of our existence was pretty much in itself, non-existent.

This all changed when we started raiding the mainlands. That is what you know as the countries of Turkey, Syria, Lebanon, Israel, and Egypt. On the mainlands they did have a highly sophisticated communication system and word of our existence did spread. Our raids upon The Hittite Empire started off as routine, the archers followed up with a massive charge. However, after about the first four or five seaside village raids, The Hittites sent their armies. These aren't ragtag bands or gangs of men that are going too be easily pushed aside. These are rigorously, well trained, well disciplined, and well armed military forces. Though swords were around by now, the choice weapon of the infantry was bronze bladed battle axes. All infantrymen were issued rawhide armor which was about as effective as wearing a sheet of plastic during a showdown in the old west. Infantrymen however was the last thing too worry about. First you had too survive the barrage of arrows being rapidly fired upon you by the oppositions archers. Not only did their archers have better armor, composite armor, which is rawhide armor covered with overlapping bronze scales, but they also had two kinds of bows. The common bow, which is just a wooden rod tapered at the ends and strung with twisted animal guts. It's accuracy range was around five hundred feet. There was also the composite bow, it was made of layers of wood and animal sinew, or muscle. It could also shoot it's arrows twice as far as the common bow. If you could survive the onslaught of these thousands of bronzed tipped missiles which seemed too blacken the sky, you only hoped and prayed that the infantry charge was next. If this was not the case your best option is too turn and flee for your life. Your odds of surviving a full fledged chariot charge were not good too say the least. They would come at you starting with a trot, but once inside a thousand feet or so they would charge, barrelling straight at you with speeds up too thirty-five miles per hour, but each chariot had not only a charioteer, they also had at least one, sometimes two archers, shooting their arrows as rapidly as possible.

The first few times we came up against this formidable enemy we not only had to retreat and flee to our ships, but we also suffered heavy casualties. This all got turned around with one tool. I say tool because even though the ancients had it they didn't think of it as a weapon. The javelin that is, used in twelve hundred B.C. primarily as a hunting weapon. We however turned it into a military weapon. After receiving the expected shower of arrows we would wait too see what is next. If it was the infantry charge we would just charge at them ourselves. If they saw fit too bring on the chariots, thousands at a time with huge clouds of dust billowing behind them. We would wait until they were close enough too launch our javelins, trying too hit one of the horses pulling the chariot. One horse is all it took too cause a chariot to violently crash. This left the chariot crew vulnerable to attack by our infantry.

Even if their chariot crew did survive, fleeing was next too impossible because of the very heavy and very awkward bronze armor they were wearing.

This innovation of ours allowed us too carry on our conquest. After the fall and defeat of The Hittites it was on to the land of Canaan. Because of perfecting our skills at the expense of The Hittites we managed too just mow over The Canaanites, who weren't as well equipped or organized as The Hittites. This took us on to Egypt. This particular campaign started off disastrous and only proceeded too get worse. Apparently by now we were quite notorious for we never saw one grain of sand of the land of Egypt. I am proud too say it was in The Mediterranean Sea, a few miles outside the East of The Nile Delta that my people, The Egyptains, brought our ancient war machine to a halt.

Oh. I'm sorry. How rude of me. Please forgive me, I have just realized that I have not properly introduced myself. I am Caesarion, however I perfer Commander Granite. You see, I am or should I say I was the only heir not too one but two empires. Two empires that were violently snatched away from me. Even though that had too be years ago by now it still somehow seems just like a few days ago. Except I was only thirteen then and I do not know how old I am today. I would guess in my early twenties. Anyhow, two empires. Arguably the two most powerful empires in the world. You see, I am the only child of both Julius Caesar and Cleopatra, therefore it was my birth right too rule The Roman Empire and Egypt. Now the death of my father, who was murdered by men he thought of as friends and allies, in March of forty-four B.C., does not bother me, but the murder of my mother, to this very moment, still angers and enrages me too the point of pure hatred for both The Roman Empire and it's so called first emporer. The same no good, lying son-of-a-bitch that stole my claim to the throne of Rome. Gaius Julius Caesar Octavianus. Other-wise known as Octavian. He would later go on too call himself Caesar Augustus, another slap-in-the-face to my heritage. Caesar is my name by birth, but Augustus comes from the month of August, which he deliberately chose in honor of the month that he murdered my mother, which through political propaganda he claimed was a suicide and that lie echoes through time too this very day.

Anyhow, I left Alexandria a few days before Octavian arrived. I fled south from Lower Egypt to Upper Egypt along the muddy banks of The Nile River toward the land of Nubia. Too distance ourselves from the impending threat that Octavian brought with him, me and my royal entourage left Alexandria with a few horse drawn chariots. Thinking we would be easier to hunt down because of these chariots, we utterly destroyed them and left the horses too fend for themselves somewhere near the twin towns of Elkab and Hierakonpolis. From here we travelled on foot to where the town of Aswan is. Except we were still on the west side of The Nile and Aswan, at that time was better known as Syene. It is here, on the west bank of The Nile River that I first encountered The Epitaph and his posse of time bandits. Even though I could tell by one look at them that they were foreigners, I had no idea just how foreign they were.

First, they were dressed in what you all would call desert camouflage. Complete with safety goggles too keep the desert sand out of their eyes. They had footwear that covered the entire foot. This was unthought of too me. Everybody in my time was either barefoot or wore sandals. Of course I would come too find out these are known as combat boots. They also had strange belts that not only carried the usual dagger but many other gizmos as well. Binoculars, a compass, a flashlight, canteen, etc... they also were carrying what I thought of as magic boom sticks that made a loud bang when activated. These boomsticks were actually guns or firearms. The forty-five caliber machine gun too be exact. These nifty toys could fire eleven point four millimeter shells at a accurate range of fifty-five yards at about four hundred rounds per minute. They also had thrity round clips and magazines and the whole thing was very light. Only about eight to ten pounds. I should point out that this was the nineteen forty-three model other wise known as a grease gun because of it's resemblance too something called a grease gun. They also had little boom sticks strapped or holstered around their waists to one side or the other. Some had them on the left, but most had them on the right. These little guns were The Schmidt Ordonnanz Revolver Model Eighteen Eighty-two, numbered, as most other firearms, after the year they were made. They could shoot six, seven point five millimeter rounds before needing reloaded. These beauties are two hundred and thirty-five millimeters long with a fixed sight at the end of the barrel. They also weigh seven hundred and fifty grams and had a dazzling walnut grip. Through The Epitaph's interpreters that could speak my language, that's Ancient Egyptian too you all, me and my allies came too understand that just as we feared The Romans were right on our tail and that Epitaph was here too rescue us. Too prove his honesty we made our way to one of the many tropical like islands that was in The Nile and waited. A few days later The Roman Legions showed up. There was no doubt too anyone why they were here. My death is all they wanted. As we spied them on the west bank from our remote island location, The Epitaph swore he could grant me revenge if I joined his cause for world domination. Of course I said yes, which leads us to where we are right now. Battling my people in The Mediterranean Sea.

As I have stated earlier, The Egyptians, under Rameses The Third, not only must have known we were coming, but had moved the capital from Thebes to Piramses in preparation of our arrival. He also had the intelligence not too let us reach land by having his navy stationed outside The Nile Delta. Thou we furiously attacked again and again with headstrong determination, in the end we were just simply outnumbered. Because of our defeat here in The Mediterranean Sea, our little venture went down in history with us being known as The Sea Peoples. If you don't believe me just check out the memorial at Medinet Habu in Egypt that Rameses quickly had erected.

Part I

The Ancients

After the success of our Mediterranean experiment we were immediately off to the next conquest. Believe me when I say too you that I thoroughly enjoyed this one, but of course I enjoy anything that involves damaging and or destroying Roman prestige and influence, which is just what we did here. In forty-three A.D. The Roman Empire started a aggressive expansion campaign into Britain or England, whichever you wish too call it. The island that would go on too be a powerful nation for quite some time was coincidentally the same island that my father considered not worthy of conquering. My father, thats Julius Caesar too all of you who were not paying attention earlier, had reached the shore of Britain in fifty-four B.C., and with very little exploration abandoned any ideas of seizing the island and instead went on to conquer Gaul or too you all in modern times, the nation of France. It took the Romans almost two decades too gain control of the island. There was however, isolated bands that did continue too resist and in sixty-one A.D., in what the Romans thought of as one, last, in vain attempt by the native inhabitants too reclaim their land and push the Roman occupiers back across the channel from where they came. That invain attempt, with our assistance, proved too be a stunning success. You see, The Iceni king, Prasutagus, died in sixty A.D. and left half of his ample sized kingdom to his wife. The other half of the kings land, unfortunately for Boudicca, the deceased kings widow, went to The Roman Emperor, Nero Claudius Drusus Germanicus, or more commonly referred too as Nero. The Emperor was a cruel tyrant who derived pleasure from the pain and suffering of others by having many elaborate public executions and beheadings. These executions only intensified after the fire of Rome in sixty-four A.D., which he decided too point his finger at, and hold responsible a group of people, who at the time in Rome, in the first century A.D., was looked down upon by mainstream Roman society. These outsiders were known as Christians. Too make the punishment fit the crime, the

Christians were not only crucified to the cross, they also were covered in tar and set ablaze in both public and private roundups as if they are human torches. Sadly and unfortunately this has nothing too do with the rebellion that led to Nero's suicide. It was his interest in literary arts such as reading, play acting, greek athletics, etc... all of which was shocking and appalling behavior too the Roman aristocracy. This mis-behavior added with his refusal too participate in basic needs of state is what led to his eventual demise.

The Iceni were one of the many celtic tribal kingdoms on the British island, who held a good size chunk of land on the east side of the island. Prasutagus must have thought that too leave half of his kingdom to The Roman Emperor ment that there would be peace between Rome and The Iceni. I for one could have, from experience, told The Iceni King "You can't trust the Romans". How does that saying go? "Give them a inch and they'll take a mile", I believe it is. That is very true where the Romans are concerned, and took a mile they did. Many of them as a matter of fact. They claimed possession of their own share then decided to help themselves to Boudicca's portion of the departed king's region. They literally marched in and seized control. When The Iceni Queen objected too this, and of course she did, she was violently beaten and eventually flogged by the Roman garrison. As if that was not insult enough, the queen's two daughters, Comorra and Tasca, were dragged before the people of the Iceni village and brutally raped again and again. I would guess that ninety percent of the Roman soldiers had their turn with the two girls. In front of everyone too witness and with no shame neither. The arrogant bastards! This naturally sent shockwaves among the celtic tribes and a few of them were all too willing to assist The Iceni Queen in her call to arms too remove their Roman oppressors. With the aid and addition of the neighboring Trinivantes, who had been living under Rome's rule for sometime now, as well as receiving brutal Roman treatment, the rebellion grew in size and strength. There was also the extra, added, support of The Calavelluni tribe. This swelled the numbers of Boudicca's fighting force to tens of thousands. Probably fifty to sixty thousand. The British Celts then started too arm themselves with spears, swords, and axes, as well as other weapons of war. When they were ready enough, the righteously hostile celtic warriors descended down upon the Roman city of Camulodunum.

Camulodunum had not only been a symbolic token of Roman culture since forty-eight A.D., but it was also ment too be a example for the barbaric tribes of Britain of what a sophisticated civilization should be. This was all the more reason for the sedition forces too despise this foreign intrusion upon their homeland. When the Celtic warriors sacked the loathed city they poured in as swiftly as a rising river would flood it's muddy banks. This wasn't too difficult since Roman commanders neglected too fortify the location with walls of any kind. Once the enraged natives besieged the city they had no mercy on the shocked and stunned inhabitants. The Celtic warriors brutally slaughtered anyone that stood before them. Most of the overwhelmed city dwellers did not even have weapons too defend themselves with when they met their bloody fate. As the Iceni swarmed into the city they set everything ablaze with the intent of destroying everything that was Roman. Homes, businesses, statues and pottery. Creatures of all kinds whether they were human or not. Those few Roman citizens that did survive had gathered in The Temple of claudius in the center of town, where they thought they would be safe. The temple was built around fifty A.D. as a dedication too Claudius and his conquest of the island. The temple was fairly large at about eighty feet wide and one hundred, five feet long. However, not even it's thick walls could save the city residences from the vengeful Iceni, who not only burnt the Roman sanctuary to a crisp pile of ashes, never too be erected again but they also, figuratively too speak, proceeded too pull out the marshmallows and hot dogs and have a giant weenie roast as those trapped in the temple let out blood curdling, high pitched, horrible screams that not only seemed to shatter your eardrums but also delighted The British Celts who now felt that some justice had been served. But this was just a taste of justice and there was no turning back now. It's either complete victory over The Romans or it was death for the Iceni. They knew that!They knew that the imperial powers of Rome would not let this go. As it turns out some of Camulodunums fleeing populace, who fled in all directions, got word to the surrounding communities. Longthorpe and Londinium were among the first. The commander of The Ninth Legion in Longthorpe immediately began the one hundred mile march south to Camulodunum. Taking with him two thousand troops and some cavalry. It would be several days before The Roman Governor of Britain, General Suetonius Paullinus, who was currently on The Island of Mona where he had just slaughtered the druids in a vicious, violent bloodbath, would become aware of the Iceni uprising, which too the governor was several hundred miles away.

The arrogance of both Rome and The Ninth Legion was working against them. The Ninth Legion was marching toward Camulodunum with over abundant confidence that they could quell and put down any barbaric revolt. They have no idea just what they are marching into. As they trotted through the lushly green woods in a single file line that stretched for miles and miles, The Iceni warriors laid their trap and sprung their ambush next to the narrow, path like road. The Iceni charged in from both sides, crunching and crushing the overwhelmed and awe struck Roman soldiers. It was a brutal massacre. The Roman Ninth Legion was slain almost down to every last man. Suetonius Paullinus was several days into his journey toward Londinium before he became aware of the slaughter of The Ninth Legion. The disbelieving shock that suddenly became apparent on the general's face, that a revolt lead by a mere woman was not only succeeding but had just annihilated a entire Roman legion was too much to take in. When he first heard that this uprising was under the direction and leadership of a mere woman he scoffed and laughed, thinking to himself, Ha!, they have women fighting for them. These people have got too be desperate. Upon hearing of the ghastly fate of The Ninth

Legion, the general now knew that this was going to be no walk threw the park. How could this have happened? By a woman!

Boudicca and the general started toward Londinium at about the same time. Suetonius, however moved as quickly as possible, where as Boudicca and her rebellious insurgency took their time by raiding and pillaging small Roman establishments along the way. Londinum, in it's young days, only about fifteen years old in sixty A.D., was usually alive with shops, traders, businessmen, and Roman officials of all kinds. However, when The Roman Governor gets there, he finds the entire populace in a hysterical uproar with justified fear that they too will soon suffer the same horrific fate as Camulodunum. Too make things worse the city's senoir official, Catus Decianus, the individual who started all of this by ordering the brutal treatment of the Iceni royal family, fled to Gaul. It does not take the enraged general long too realize that Londinum can not be defended or saved. He takes all the men and teenage boys that could fight and leaves the rest to their own demise. Women, children, sick, old, dying, telling these people to flee the city. Some do and of course some do not. It was only a mere few hours after being abandoned by the general that the Roman city was sacked and destroyed. The unforgiving Iceni eradicated and exterminated anything and everything. Completely liquidating the Roman metropolis of Londinum far worse than that of Camulodunum. The residents were brutally tortured and mutilated. Cut to little, unrecognizable pieces, and in some instances it was sometimes worse than that. Just like Camulodunum, Londinium was also set ablaze and reduced to a pile of rubble. Archaeologists, even in your time can still find proof of the utter carnage inflicted upon the city by Boudicca and her horde of rebels. A completely burnt layer of Earth, not too far into the ground.

I, as you have probably noticed, have made several references too your time and/or your era. I should clarify that if my calculations are correct this publication will first be available sometime in the early twenty-first century. It is too these people that I am referring too when I say your time or your era.

After the sacking and destruction of Londinium, modern day London, just as Camulodunum is modern day Colchester, the Iceni scouts came in with reports that the Roman army was moving north along the main Roman road of Watling Street. Watling street was originally a wet and very muddy foot and cart path used by the celts long before the Romans intruded on the British people. By sixty A.D. however, the Romans had paved the road and used it primarily for military purposes. Paving roads was a art the Romans had perfected long ago. Centuries in fact. All Roman roads had the same basic structure, depending on location and the materials available for construction. Roman roads started off by being dug about three feet into the ground. They are then filled with large gravel and sand, topped by a layer of pebbles and smaller gravel that is then leveled. From here, most Roman roads went directly to the top layer, that is usually cobblestone or pavement of flat, hard stones with concrete or pebbles set in mortar. Not only are these streets thirteen too twenty-three feet wide but they are also sloped from the center so that the rain will flow into the ditches that straddled both sides of these highways. Anyhow, the Iceni decided too give immediate pursuit too the Roman forces traveling up Watling Street. Once again, the Roman forces advance with abrupt speed while the British natives plundered many Roman colonies along the way, including the Roman stronghold of Verulamium, modern day Saint Albans.

After finding himself just south of Wales, General Suetonius very tactically choose his spot for a battlefield, and since he was a few days ahead of Boudicca, the choice was his too choose. It was a spot not only with a slight incline to his back, but also well wooded with many trees on three sides and a narrow opening in front of him. Now all he and his men had too do was patiently wait, and that is far easier said than done. One tends too get a little jittery while lingering around, anticipating the up and coming confrontation. Knowing that some of your comrades around you would soon not be there. And who knows, you might not be there either. However, not only did Suetonius deliberately keep his men busy with calisthenics and military exercises, there was also the work of setting up camp and preparing for the battle. When days later the Iceni finally arrived, not only had Boudicca's force swelled to about a quarter million people, but because of their overwhelming success and string of uninterrupted victories the Brits' were hysterically jubilant with the feeling that they were going too completely be rid of these Roman occupiers. Lucky for them we were nearby. Well hidden and well concealed, dressed in our modern day military camouflage. In fact we had been in hiding and waiting even days before the Romans showed up. So it was we who had the leisure of sitting back and watching the battle unfold in front of us. Epitaph, as usual had given me strict orders as when too intervene. He seldom though gave me orders as too how, but he would however encourage and even reward us for large amounts of excessive, brutal violence. He wanted it too be well thought and believed that we were some kind of plague allowed to roam free by Gods anger. The Army of Darkness if you would like, which is what we eventually came too be known as by some.

We really didn't have too put forth much of a effort too achieve this. The ear-shattering sonic boom that proceeded our arrival could be heard for five miles and seen even further. Then the sudden appearance out of a fog like haze, of at least tens, usually hundreds of thousands of marching troops, mainly equipped with your modern technology, that also could be heard before seen. Whether it be the thunderous rumbling of horses hoofs or the cacophonous roaring of battle tanks and other motorizied equipment, if you were someone living in ancient ages up to mideval times and just so happened too witness this spectacle take place in front of your very eyes, with your limited understanding of science, and I speak with experience, don't forget I was supposed too die in thirty B.C. at the hands of Roman legionaries, and since meeting Epitaph I not only have been awakend by the wonders of your world but I know people of my time would never have believed possible what you take for granted. Anyhow, if you were too stand there when we come forth from our smoky cover, sometimes with our anti-chemical weapon suits, which we would wear not only for shock and terror, but too awe our enemy with something that did not look quit human. You would have very easily believed that we were demons from hell allowed by God too play. With our firearms that would reach right over and pluck your life from afar. Mortar shells raining down on you from high above. Thats not forget the thousands of grenades being simultaneously hurled at you. All of this would make you a very sudden believer. In my time, when a natural disaster, such as a earthquake or tsunami happened it was already blamed on the angry gods. So what else would they blame a phantom army on. A army that seemed too appear out of nowhere and swiftly return from whence it came.

Back at The Watling Street battlefield, and after a night of setting camp across from one another the two armies were preparing too square off. With their military formations set in place, each commander proceeded to give their troops a inspirational, motivational pep talk. Boudicca pointing out that the Britions greatly outnumber the cowering Romans who hide behind their shields, by about five to one. Suetonius was telling his men too keep their nerve and no matter what too hold steady their battle formations. The fact that the British have made it this far he said "... is a insult too everything Roman, just look across the field. Our opponents are mainly women" "WOMEN!". Which was not an exaggeration by any stretch of the mind. The English had brought everybody. Aunts, uncles, nieces, nephews, even their children wanted too witness the great victory that was about too take place. The Brits' were ready, and what a motley looking sight they made. With their long frizzed hair that seemed too go any which way but down. The blue woad body paint that they used too decorate themselves with in a variety of different designs. The fact that they would yell and scream at the top of their lungs while banging their swords and shields together. Whipping themselves and each other into a frantic frenzy.

If, on the other side of the field, the Romans were afraid of this barbaric display of force, they did a good job of not letting it show. They held fast and kept their nerve just as their general had ordered. The Romans were equipped with the very latest first century body armor. Lorica Segmentata. Flexible steel with overlapping plates that covered their torso and shoulders, no weapon the celts had would be able too penetrate it. However, if a warrior knew where to strike at with his sword there was a few weak spots in the armor design. Such as the armpits or neck area, maybe even a lucky thrust between the overlapping armor plates themselves. Next the Roman soldier would be wearing a steel helmet, complete with built-in neck guard, probably of Gallic origin. They would be wearing sandals as well as carrying a scutum, or shield. The scutum was a rectangler piece of wood bounded in brass around the entire edge and covered with rawhide the rest of the way. It was about forty-two inches high and about five to six millimeters thick. The rounded curve that protruded from the shield itself, not only protected the entire body but also allowed the Roman soldier too absorb massive enemy blows.

Now the fighting between these two forces commenced, starting with a barbaric British charge. The frighteningly savage looking Brits' running full steam ahead at the Romans were met with thousands of Roman pilum, or javelins as you would call them. Theses pilum smashed right through the celtic forces and completely decimated their first few ranks. Unfortunatley for the celts, the Romans always carried two pilum. Since Boudicca's force was so numerous this did little too slow the island natives down. Another wave of warriors were there too fill the empty slots almost immediately. Now that the Romans had discharged their pilum it was time too take the brunt of what the celts had too offer. As the celts burst up the field with a fresh charge, the Romans set their shieldwall formation. Each soldier standing shoulder to shoulder holding their scutums at about mid-level while simultaneously overlapping the shield of the man next too him so that everyone benefitted, not only from the protection of his own shield but also his neighbour's shield as well. When the winded celts crashed into this shieldwall upon their arrival to the Roman side of battle, the Romans with the use of their shields, would absorb whatever form of attack that the particular celtic warrior in front of him had brought. It didn't matter what weapon the celts yielded. Sword, axe, spear, etc..., the Roman scutum would take the impact of the blow. Then, the Roman soldier with the use of his shieldboss would violently assault his attacker, shoving him brutally to the ground, only too be followed up with the thunderous thud that echoed threw your body when contact too the Earth was made. Only providence knew if you would look up in time too avoid that short sword the Roman soldier was bearing down at you with.

Upon completion of a successful shieldboss thrust the Gladius would come into play. Gladius Hispaniensis. The favored weapon of The Roman soldier. A short little stubby sword that is excellent for stabbing and gutting your opponent. It originated from the Iberian Peninsula and probably was acquired by Rome around two thirty-five B.C., this type of sword was approximately thirty inches long from capulus to tip and weighed one point six kilograms. It also was crafted with a wooden handle that had been sanded down to a smooth surface. A lot of Roman soldiers would wrap leather or rawhide around the hilt of the sword or their hands for a much better grip when sticking you in the abdomen and pulling your innards out to the ground. Soaking the Earths floor in your blood and guts.

After withstanding many bellowing Celtic charges, the Roman soldiers started too take the initiative by pressing and pushing forward. The front line soldiers would shove their shields into the grills of their opponents following with a savage thrust of his sword while simultaneously taking short, gradual steps in a onward direction. Now bearing down and driving the Brits back by stepping on and over the thousands of Celtic warriors that lie dead and dying on the Watling Street battlefield, the Roman soldiers slowly gain the upper hand. However a frontline soldier could only do this for so long, but you know them crafty Romans. They had a admirable solution for this minor problem. Constant rotation. Behind each frontline Roman soldier was seven more of his comrades in arms and when he moved forward, they all moved forward. All in unisync with each other as if they were one great big, giant, semi-human, half machine being. After about eight minutes of this, the soldier who was immediately behind the frontline trooper would move up just as his amigo was stepping back to the rear of the pack, only too make his way back up front sixty-four minutes from now. After this carried on for quite some time the real Roman aggression was about too commence. The order was given for the wedge formation "Clausus e former" the general would repeatedly be yelling to his troops. Over and over, again and again. He knew that his men would have a hard time hearing him over the clanging of weapons, yelling of unfortunate souls clinging percariously to life, the thunderous pounding of horses hoofs and the squeaky wagons they were dragging behind them. But the Romans are a very disciplined military unit. A unit were each individual man knew his exact position in line and his specifically assigned task at hand. A unit that heard their generals orders.

The wedge formation was more than just a continuous line of troops in the form of many triangles, but all the Roman troops were packed in close together like peas in a can, bulldozing all their weight against the Iceni forces, trapping them in the corners of the formation and pushing them back to the side of the battlefield from where they came. The Romans press on, never letting up. Shoving the Iceni warriors further and further back. Little by little, step by step, the Romans march down the field, beating back Britains as they make their way to the other side of the combat zone. When Suetonius Paullinus noticed that the Britains were turning to flee, he set free his cavalry reserves who just plow right through Iceni troops, slashing down enemy personal on their pursuit to the next victim. Releasing the cavalry really was not necessary, because as the Iceni soon discovered, they had sealed their own fate before the first angry thrust had ever been thrown at a enemy soldier.

The Iceni had set-up camp the night before by arranging all their wagons in a protective, horseshoe like semi-circle. This is where all the celtic noncombatants, mainly young children and the elderly had stayed too witness the great celtic victory they soon expected too take place. What they didn't expect was the mad rush of incoming, and fleeing, Iceni warriors. Warriors who were trying to outrun the pursuing Roman legions but could find nowhere to go. The wagons had been crammed so close together that not even a child's body could squeeze through to the other side, to the other side for possible safety. It seems now that the protective semi-circle is currently getting all Iceni, both combatants and noncombatants, killed dead by our Roman adversaries. That's right. Our Roman adversaries. The island natives are about too recieve some much needed help from myself and the rest of The Army of Darkness. It was just as the full weight of the mighty Roman army was bearing down on the Iceni warriors that we sprang our trap and sprung from the trees running the entire length of the left and right sides of the field of battle. The Roman soldiers were so focused on their Celtic prey that they hadn't even noticed us stepping out from the thick, dense woods with trees so compacted and compressed together that sunlight would hardly penetrate to the forest floor. It would almost be like stepping into a deep, dark cave. Even at high noon. The first of our troops too make their appearance on the chaotic field of battle were the grenadiers. Approaching from both flanks and from behind the Iceni wagon train, the grenadiers were equipped with the standard issue camouflage trousers and jackets. Concealed beneath the camouflage jackets are the flak jackets. These are the very ones that will be issued too the western allies during world war two. They are very heavy due too the fact that these jackets are multi-layered nylon with thick steel plates sewn into the center of them. Even though these flak jackets are not ment too be worn by ground troops over long distances, they are ment too stop fast flying metal pieces of flak shrapnel. Flak, as in german anti-aircraft flak. Flak, as in "Oh shit, I wouldn't be alive if I didn't have this flak jacket on". They were even effective at stopping small arms fire from hand-held weapons. All this made them perfect for our uses, as they would stop any projectile or sharp, pointy weapon the Romans would wield against us. Their arrows and pila would literally bounce right off, and if a Roman actually got close enough too thrust his sword at one of us he would be in for a shocking surprise when his thrusting blade would suddenly stop with a thud as a result of striking one of those many steel plates I had just mentioned a few sentences ago. He would be dead long before he ever figures out why he struck something solid instead of gutting another nameless victim of the Roman army. The grenadiers would also be carrying the standard issue Epitaph dagger of war along with the small arm of choice for this particular operation. The Remington Model Eighteen Fifty Eight New Army Percussion revolver is a beaut. A real handy piece of work. True art if I ever saw it. At thirteen point twenty-five inches long this six-shot, single-action, forty-four caliber pistol not only had a fixed sight at the barrel end and walnut grip plates, but it's stong closed frame was topped with a octagonal barrel.

Now I know some of you are thinking, Caesarion, what does single action mean too me? Well, just sit back and allow me too tell you. There are two types of action. Single and double. Single means that you have too manually pull the hammer back yourself before pulling the trigger. I realize thats a little too hard for you twenty-first centurions with your cell-phones strapped too your waist like your in the old wild west of America, but please, try too work with me. If you were in the old wild west you would want a double action revolver, just like the one your already accustomed too. The one where all you do is just pull the trigger.

Now the most important thing the grenadiers would have with them was, yes, thats right, the grenades. Our grenadiers are carrying the flaming ceramic jars that would first see battle action in the mid-seven hundreds A.D. by the fearful Byzantine Empire, or as I always refer to them as "The Eastern Roman Empire." Thats really what they are. The leftovers of The Roman Empire. In two eighty five A.D. the emperor Diocletian decided too divvy up the empire into two halves, even though in name it is still one empire, this is where the distinction between Eastern and Western Roman Empire became a reality, however the impact was truely felt a few decades later when Constantinople, a city in The Eastern Roman Empire, became the capital city of the entire Roman Empire. So in four seventy six A.D., when The Western Roman Empire fell too barbarian invaders, thus was born The Byzantine Empire. However Byzantine Emperors considered themselves as successors of The Roman Empire and repeatedly tried too reclaim all the lands of the once mighty Roman Empire. Now back too our ceramic jar grenades. They are just jars of fire that explode and break apart upon impact after hitting the target and spreading the fire all about, thus creating many small fires that will spread and grow very quickly. Like spontaneous torches springing forth from the bowels of the Earth. These fires, as these particular Roman soldiers are about too find out, not only are very difficult too put out but also seems too stick right too you. Almost like wet mud or thick syrup. This is a concoction known as greek fire.

Greek fire, consisting mainly of petroleum, sulfur, saltpeter, and other such ingredients that I can't divulge here on these pages, is a very deadly and effective weapon. So effective that not only would water not put the fire out, it actually helped spread the fire even more. Being in the open water against this tool of war is a real pain in the ass, as greek fire will literally float on the waters surface. This is a good thing, as this caused the Byzantines too limit their use of this weapon, because they too had to traverse the surface water fires that they themselves were creating. However, greek fire, in a jar, on land is, in my opinion, far worse than greek fire at sea. At least on water you might be able to maneuver around this obstacle but on land, it spreads quickly, too everything. Grass, bushes, shrubs, trees, clothes, people, etc... Thats not a problem. My boys can chunk these things from a safe distance of about one hundred feet away from the Roman enemy, and if their the ones on fire, lets make a toast and have a drink.

The Roman army, thanks too their loyal discipline and fear of their generals, continued to march forward toward the grenaders, as they were hacking down helpless Iceni victims when the first flaming jars rained down upon them, as if the god of brimstone and fire flew by and spewed them from his mouth. Even as the jars came down and Roman soldiers burst into flames, falling to the ground while screaming in agonizing pain, their fanatical comrades pressed on, blindly loyal too the bloody end. Luckily, for the Roman enemy, the grenadiers could only carry two flaming jars at a time. With one thousand grenadiers per line, and three lines per position, and three positions, that would be eighteen thousand incoming flaming greek fire jars on the Roman side of battle, and still they bravely keep coming!When the grenadiers are finished discharging their lethal, hand held jars of fire, they then fall back to their secondary positions, behind The Epitaph Rifle Division.

The rifle division would also be wearing standard camouflage trousers and jackets complete with flak jackets and The Epitaph Dagger of War. Yes, they even had The Remington Model Eighteen Fifty Eight New Army Percussion Revolver strapped to their waist just like your cell phone. The difference being that instead of carrying flaming jars of greek fire, the rifle division is armed with the Berdan Two bolt action rifle. The Berdan Two is a breech loading, single shot, forty- two caliber infantry rifle that will be standard issue in the Russian army from eighteen seventy to eighteen ninety-one. It was created by American firearms expert Hiram Berdan and will see global action clear up to the end of world war two. It is well known for it's accuracy, simplicity, and reliability. Why else do you think we are using them?

By now we had the attention of the Roman soldiers and when they looked our way they found themselves looking straight into about one thousand Berdan Two barrels. Fortunately for them we only brought four and a-half battallions. Our whole division is about fifteen thousands troops. Fifteen thousand Berdan Two barrels. Soon the battlefield erupted with the sound of firearms. A sound no Roman has ever heard before. A sound that made these Romans stop dead in their tracks. The greek fire clay jars didn't even phase those fortunate Romans that didn't burst into flames, but when they noticed their Roman brothers dropping down dead without being touched by a sword, axe, or other blunt object, they knew it had something too do with this new foreign noise that had just startled the beegeebees out of them and they did the one thing that no Roman does no matter what! They turned to flee. The sight of almost one thousand of their comrades in arms just dropping down dead to the ground, in what in their minds was both impossible and god like was just too much too take in. Who were these strangers? What was that thunderous noise, and how could these people work such magic? They must be in league with Lucifer! Thats just a few of the thoughts skipping through the minds of these Romans, but the thoughts of their commanders were far different. Yes, the general and his aids heard the thunderous boom of the Berdan Two and even though they could not visually see the source of this deafing, ear-splitting sound. The general did visually see his forces break their formations and dart across the field, tossing their weapons and gear aside in a invain attempt too save their worthless Roman hides. Through all the chaos, confusion, and madness with dirt and dust now hovering through-out the air, the sound of men screaming and yelling, horses neighing, rifles barking out their breath of fire as the bullets would fly threw the air. Not one, no-good, good-for-nothing, worthless Roman soldier ever heard a damn word the general was wildly yelling. He had yet failed too realize that the time too cut your loses and get out of Dodge was long since past. The Roman soldiers however were well aware of that fact and well on their way back to their side of the field, where their camp was still set-up, but that was just a mere detail as they probably right about now are finding out.

Epitaph infantry troops are pouring into the battle from both sides of the field. All along the edges of the battlefield, where the flat terrain meets the wooded forest, our foot soldiers are swiftly rushing out too encircle and cut-down Roman troops as they try too reach safety. Ha! What were they thinking? Safety! There is no such thing when your as surrounded and outnumbered as they are. In their little corner, about where their camp sat. The Roman soldiers made a valiant last stand. Well..., they tried. Just too make things feel like a fair, sporting event, after the Romans broke and ran we mostly used first century weapons too cut them down. Weapons that they would recognize.

I know a lot of you have never stepped foot onto a first century battlefield, but after the conflict comes the gruesome task of cleaning up. Amputated limbs and appendages lie littered all over the ground. The ground itself is difficult too stand upon as it was so drenched and slicked with blood that splashed half-way up your calves with each step that you take. The smell of blood and death is so foul and wretched that you would be wishing you didn't have nostrils too breath with. Bodies, with or without all their arms and legs were strewn everywhere. It's a sight you only want too see if your passing threw hell. We helped those few Iceni warriors who returned, bury their dead. They became curious of us when they noticed that we ran past them but gutted every Roman scum we saw. Because of this they were more than eager too become our friends. They knew that on this day they almost lost Briain.

Finally, the time had come for diplomatic relations. This means that at last I get too meet the well celebrated and beloved queen of the Iceni herself, Boudicca. She is pure beauty itself. Living art, walking poetry, animated grace. The queen herself is a magnificent specimen standing at nearly six feet tall, and as most Celts, towers over her Roman adversaries. Her bright, auburn hair, which flowed like fields of cotton down to her waist, seemed too glisten when she stood in the sunlight. She was decorated, as a queen should be, with many bright ornaments. Gold and silver chains adorned her neck while bronze braces ran up her arms. She also wore many rings on her fingers and a touch of blue woad was still on her face. When she spoke, her voice commanded respect. The queen and I came too an agreement that all of Britain is too now be garrisoned by Army of Darkness troops in order too stop The Romans and other would be invaders. It wasn't too hard too convince her that when the Romans find out what happened too their British troops that they will send more. In our appreciation of her defiance of the Romans, she and the rest of the Iceni will rule England as they see fit, and if need be, we will be the muscle behind her throne. However, the Iceni, when need be, must give their service too The Army of Darkness. A strong alliance was formed here today.

Now I know what your thinking, and don't worry. General Suetonius Paullinus did not get away. In southern England, where a lone Roman camp sits. The commander of the Second Legion, who had willingly disobeyed Suetonius's order too join him in a pitched battle against the Celts, was surprised too be recieving reports of what appeared too be another messenger from Suetonius. He is a Roman messenger. The only Roman who survived The Watling Street slaughter, and the message he brings to the commander of the Second Legion is Suetonius's bloody stump of a head in a basket and a verbal order too leave the island or suffer the same fate as the late general. The commander, in the middle of a nervous breakdown, honorably decided too commit suicide, and the poor fellow who succeeded him foolishly choose too fight. I guess I don't have too tell you how that ended.

When, back in Rome, the emperor recieved the package that held the now foul smelling cranium of the general. Nero was appalled and horrified that barbarians would have the audacity too do such a thing. And too top it all off, these barbarians are lead by a woman. A WOMAN! The mighty Roman Empire would not stand for this. Most troops of the empire where summoned to a rallying point somewhere in western Gaul too finally put an end too this barbaric madness that had recently consumed the province of Britain. Roman military commanders, acting without Nero must have thought that too send the vast majority of their military might against our celtic allies would cause them too fold like a lawn chair in the wind. The Celts never knew of the Romans intentions, as the Romans never even made it across the English Channel. After a few nights of outrages feasts and fiestive celebrations with our new found Celtic friends, and a new base of operations on the British mainland, we recieved Epitaph's orders as to where our next mission will lead us.

When, back in Rome, the military commanders came too discover the horrific fate of their ill-fated forces that were lost at sea they were truly shocked. Rome has not suffered a set-back like this since Boiorix, since Surena, since Brennus, since Hannibal Barca!

If you are a Roman, Hannibal Barca is truly the stuff that nightmares are made of. A real boogeyman. A menace too civil societies such as the one the Romans fancied themselves too have. A society where the aristocratic wealthy dined on stuffed roasted doormice and thought it proper etiquette too regurgitate during dining. I mean yuck! Gross me out. Now I want too regurgitate.

Hannibal's father was a very renowned and respected Carthaginian general who not only ruthlessly clashed and brawled against the Romans during the long, drawn-out, first punic war, but only withdrew his undefeated forces after those spinless politicians back home signed consessions to the Roman government. Consessions that only went from bad to worse.

Hannibal had scourged and terrorized the landscape of Rome for almost fifteen years. Wandering around at will while decimating every army that Rome could muster against him. Sacking Roman towns and settlements throught-out the Italian peninsula, and even though the Romans continued too lose battle after battle they refused too surrender too this Carthaginian monstrosity that permeated their every fears. It was unroman too except defeat, especially from a real nightmare that materialized into a life of it's own, except his name isn't Freddy and there is no Elm street in Rome. Yeah, thats right! I'm hip too twentieth century sub-culture. What do you think I do in my free time? Figure-skating! Hannibal could win battles, but he lacked the strength to sack the city of Rome itself. The one event that would bring Rome to it's knees and force their capitulation, but it was not ment too be. The

Romans adopted a fighting without fighting policy. War of attrition, by following the enemy and denying them supplies. Burn crops, divert streams, block paths and roads, anything too slow up the opposition and keep them from food and more weapons, but no head-on battles, no matter what! After about six years of this, the Republic unfortunately regained it's strength and moral by going on the offensive against both Hannibal and the nation of Carthage itself. This all culminated in North Africa in the battle of Zama with the first, only, and final defeat of Hannibal Barca. Rome, as usual, somehow found a way too persevere. However, not even Rome could have predicted the eventual rise and return of Hannibal once again.

After his defeat at Zama, Hannibal took a lengthy hiatus from public life too collect and gather his thoughts on how lifes fortunes can turn so very quickly. One moment your euphorically on the up and up and the next moment it's being stripped from the tight grip of the palm of your hand. After a few years of reclusively hibernating, Hannibal decided too throw his perverbial helmet into the political circle and was expeditiously elected as chief magistrate. It didn't last long though. It only took a few years for Rome too become alarmed by Hannibal's high political power and status. It only took Rome a few years too fear a Carthage resurgance. A Carthage resurgance with Hannibal at the helm. This was something Rome could not tolerate, in any way. When Hannibal became aware that Rome had dispatched troops for his arrest he fled east from Carthage, never to return to his homeland again. Hannibal sought refuge in the Seleucid Empire, which at that time is ruled by Antiochus the Third, who quickly named Hannibal chief military advisor and commander of the navy, but Hannibal's military genius was that of a land general and as commander of the navy he was like a fish out of water. As military advisor his advice was often ignored and as a result, Antiochus, who even before Hannibal arrived was locked in a fierce power struggle against Rome, was soundly defeated. This was not good for Hannibal. One of the stipulations that Rome put on Antiochus was that he turn Hannibal over too them.

Hannibal, once again fled from the Roman sphere of reach, living his life on the run for many years with the Roman army in relentless pursuit. Hounding him like you would a cunning game fox. This all culminated in the Kingdom of Bithynia. Bithynia, located off of the southern shore of the pontus Euxinus, oh, i'm sorry, thats the Black Sea too you twenty-first centurions, was a land of monstrous mountains, plush fertile valleys, and lushes of forested areas with many vastly different types of trees.

One eighty three B.C., the court of Prusias The First. Hannibal had actually been seeking refuge here for a few years by now and was kind of surprised too find that the king had betrayed him by selling him out too the Romans, but even he was thinking he should have known. Hannibal, in his private chambers, that was dark and gloomy even during the brightest of days, was even more so now that dusk is rapidly approaching, stood over a small wooden table mixing the poison with which he intended too take his life with. "Why do that, when their is Romans too be defeated?" I asked as I stepped from the shadows. The tourches on the walls illuminated the big man as he quickly spun around, scanning the darkness as he searched for the source of my voice. "Who are you, and what is your purpose here?" The tall Carthaginian rudely demanded. By now I had revealed myself by stepping into what little artificial light their was. "Commander Granite, and i'm here to give you victory!" I sternly stated. "Commander of what?" Was Hannibal's sarcastic reply. "The Army of Darkness, Beelzebub's Boys, Hades Heroes, Diablo's daredevil's, whatever you wish too call us." I answered. "That is myths and legends my friend. Stories with which too scare little children." He retorted. "How do you explain my sudden appearance, seemingly out of nowhere?" I asked as I gazed in his direction. "We both know that Roman soldiers draw near as we speak, with the intention of taking you away, so you can either believe me, wait too die at their hands, or drink your poison, which do you want?" Time was not of the essence here, nor was it on our side, but I had too make Hannibal understand this fact. "What if I said I could work a miracle for you. Give you a second chance too change a injustice that was bestowed upon you by our enemy, The Romans." I pressed on, trying too arouse his curiosity. "And what do you know of the Romans?" he snapped. "Like you, I know how too defeat them in battle, so that's go before we find ourselves crucified before the city gates." I snapped back. "Go where, Prusias's guards are all over this place. We would never get out of the palace, let alone off of the grounds, and you yourself acknowledge that Roman troops are on their way here, who's going too stop them, the two of us?" His voice was raising as he stepped ever closer. It was now that I could finally see that not only was Hannibal almost six feet tall, very large for second century B.C., but he was still physically stong for a sixty-four year old man who by now had been wearing a eye patch for several years. Though the Romans thought of him as a black man he was by far not what you would call 'ace of spades black'. He was more of a bronze color, such as myself.

I gave the signal by raising my hand, and my men stepped out of the shadows as well. I am being accompanied by both battle troops and Epitaph Time Travel technicians. Time travel technicians are lightly armed troops, and being that the time travel transporters are usually built with-in eyesight of the frontlines, with bombs, grenades, rapid gun fire, and who knows what else exploding all around them, they have become quick and efficient at putting together the time travel transporters. Scurrying around like busy little mice who have just stolen the cheese out of the trap and are desparetly trying too outrun the pursing feline, collectively en masse, they slap these hulking, husky machines together. After making all the necessary adjustments, and flipping the correct switches, the time travel transporter is fired up and ready to go. Just how it works, well, nevermind, we don't have time for that here, but, don't worry, i'll later on explain in greater detail what little I do understand of how this futuristic contraption functions, but for now we have too get Hannibal out of Prusias's stronghold of a palace. Being that the time travel transporters emit huge amounts of raw power it should go without saying, but i'll say it anyway, they are very load. Ear-splitting load. In fact everyone, myself included, has too wear big, bulky, earplugs that cover the entire side of a individuals face. Prusias's palace guards heard the commotion of the time travel transporters. The sound of the raw power that runs these futuristic machines, in Hannibal's chambers, but by the time they busted in the door, all that remained of our presence was a thick, stenchy, cloud of foul smelling smoke and blackened, chared, scorch marks, left all over the walls. Not only were we gone, but Hannibal as well. Too Prusias's guards it was as if Hannibal just disappeared without a trace. Of course, Prusias's confussed guards were looking around in stunned amazement, wondering what could have caused so much smoke. And the walls. How did they become so black. Black as night. Black as pitch darkness.

Hannibal was shocked when he realized where he was, knowing that he had been here before. A little over three decades ago that is. He knew that he is standing on The Italian peninsula. The homeland of those wretched Romans. That he isn't to far from the heart of Rome itself. What he didn't know is that he is currently standing right smack in the middle of thirty years ago. The year is two zero seven B.C., and we are somewhere east of a little unknown settlement named Fossombrone. Fossombrone, built on the ruins of The Forum Semproni Roman Urban Centre, is a small community nestled in the slopes of the steep, majestic mountains that make the little village appear as if it was built too house elves or dwarfs. On the top of Sant' Aldebrando hill, centuries from now, will sit the rotting ruins of The Malatestian Feltresca Fortresses built by the Malatesta family who, in the fourteenth century A.D. will come too dominate Rimini and the surrounding areas including Fossombrone. Extending their rule as far south as Ascoli. However, as I stated, we are east of all of this. East of the mountains, east of the dwarf village that you miss if you blink while passing by. East of the splendid, marvelous river that graciously flows past this scenic view. Where we stand the rough, jagged mountains have morphed into gently rolling hills and the river. It still flows by, just not quite as graciously. We are on the north side of the river, a handful of miles west of The Adriatic Sea, and dusk is rapidly approaching. From where we stood, looking through a high powered twentieth century telescope, which Hannibal was amazed by, I pointed out too him where the Roman campsite was located. I told him that tomarrow we destroy the Romans and that in the process of doing so, he will witness the miracle I promised him.

As you might expect, I rose bright and early the next day, stationing my troops where they needed to be. I say troops because Epitaph taught me too do things the modern way. Your modern way, and as a result my troops consist of anybody between the ages of thirteen and death, no matter what their gender. If they can point a firearm and pull the trigger, they're welcomed in this army, and thats about the only qualification there is. Though to advance beyond the infantry level you do need higher training, but we have our own modern school system. Your modern school system. Anyhow, a little while later, me and Hannibal were spying on the Roman camp through the telescope again. They had expeditiously dismantled the campsite of the night before and were now in the act of preparing for battle. I was explaining too Hannibal that the Romans had gathered intelligence that had led them too believe that their enemy would be passing right through here on the very spot that they are occupying. What I didn't tell the good size Carthaginian is that the Romans were allowed this intelligence through devious deception by me and some of my cohorts, and that they were allowed this information so that they would step into the trap that was about too be sprung on them.

I was mistakenly telling Hannibal that we probably had a hour or two before the vicious fun would begin when behold, the Romans intended victims came trotting into sight. What a spectacle of a scene they were. The Iberians with their small, round shields and short curved swords that they loudly banged together while simultaneously yelling and screaming at the top of their lungs. The same as the rest of the nationally unified forces in a attempt to scare and frighten the pint size Romans. They wore white tunics with a purple border along the sleeves and neck. They also wore bronze helmets that had been dusted and dented with many years of abuse. Like their celtic partners, they towered over the short Roman adversaries. Many of the Celtic warriors were not only fighting shirt-less, but also wore woad tattoos depicting various different deities and likes of the such. Both the Iberians and celts also contributed cavalry forces too the anti-roman cause, but the cream-of-the-crop or the elite of the pack is by far the Numidian cavalry. Their horses are smaller and there-fore they are faster. Nor are they weighed down by a saddle or horse armor. They, like the Iberians, also carry small round shields. Unlike the Spaniards, they also carry a twelve foot spear and a short sword. In front of the highly prized Numidian cavalry is the spearmen. Originating from somewhere in Africa, the spearmen are armed with, yep, you guessed it, a spear. They wore red tunics. Many of them also had on Roman chainmail and helmets that probably also were of Roman origin. They had round hoplite like shields, that when held up, stretched from the middle of their chins to the middle of their knees. The Africans also preferred too fight in a phalanx formation.

The phalanx, at one time was a very formidable style of combat. Almost unstoppable in a straight, head-on confrontation, however completely helpless if flanked or encircled. The phalanx relied on the strength of it's close formation and the length of the pikes it's members wielded. Once the two armies clashed, face to face, the gallant bravery of the first three too five ranks of men, though important is almost inconsequential without the support of the following ranks of troops. It's the men in the rear that made the real difference as too what the outcome of battle would be. Oh sure, it sounds like they have the simple part, only having to push with all their might onto their comrades in front. You and the sweat laden, stinky soldiers around yourself having to press your sweaty, unbathed, smelly body against your comrades as you push the men in front of you onward to victory. Pushing and pressing with everything you have.

Knowing you can't stop until victory is achieved. And how long did this have to go on? Thirty, forty minutes. Possibly longer. A ordinary man such as yourself would give out after about ten minutes, so I don't want too hear about those chumps in the back who are piggy backing a victory off of the real men up front. The real men upfront know that victory isn't possible without those chumps in the back. Hannibal's jaw quickly hit the dirt on the ground as realization dawned as too what his visual optics were beholding. He immediately knew that he was laying his eyes on a genuine Carthaginian army. A Carthaginian army that didn't exsist.

BOOM! Flashback! For all of you who zoned out earlier, Hannibal suffered his only military defeat previously at Zama. As a result of that said defeat, Carthage was prohibited from ever having a army of any kind. Yet somehow the Carthaginian general has found himself looking at just such a army. Wait till he discovers that it's two zero seven B.C. instead of one eighty three B.C. Hannibal, with a dumbfound look on his face, turned to me and asked "Did Carthage renew the war against Rome?" "You could say that." I replied.

The two opposing forces were equally surprised too find themselves gazing at one another. The Romans had still been in the process of making their pre-battle preparations when the Carthaginians came strolling into view. Even though it didn't take them feculent Romans long at all too give chase. The two Roman commanders, Marcus Livius Solinator and Gaius Claudius Nero weren't quick enough. The stunned Carthaginians were able to fall back much more swiftly than the Romans could pursue. This gave them time too prepare a make-shift defense as well as something that looked like a front line. Immediately Hannibal and I sprang into action, sprinting toward the closest puddle jumper.

Puddle jumper! What you know as the American jeep of world war two, is a quarter ton, four by four, with a four cylinder, water cooled engine with speeds up too fifty plus miles per hour and a standard three-speed transmission. It also has a fifteen gallon gas tank, that unfortunately for the operator is directly under the driver seat. It also, believe it or not, comes with a standard issue m-one garand rifle and emergency air hand-pump. My favorite feature of this vehicle is that the headlights actually flip-out and shine down on the engine for nighttime repairs. Not that you would need too use them. I mean come on, this is a tough little buggy, deriving it's name from the character featured in a nineteen thirty-six episode of the popular popeye cartoon, that seemed able to go anywhere and do anything. We love these mechanical chariots and use a lot of them as well as their opposition counterpart the Kubelwagon. The Kubelwagon or bucket-seat car made by Ferdinand Porsche is a rear wheel drive with a four-speed transmission, however it doesn't have four-wheel drive. Depending on what year model you have it has either a air cooled, nine hundred eighty-five c.c. engine or a one thousand one hundred thirty-one c.c. engine which is located in the rear of the vehicle. What you would think of as the trunk. Even though these beauts' were field tested in the nineteen thirty-nine invasion of Poland, they, like the jeep, didn't go into full production until nineteen forty. Their were over fifty thousand of these land roving vehicles made. Not even a sixth of how many jeeps were produced. By the look on Hannibals face I knew he thought me a little crazy for hopping into what he thought of as a horse-less carriage. After all, he had never seen one before, but he loves them now and uses them quite often. He didn't hesitate, jumping in right after me. With myself behind the wheel, we bounced across the landscape, jolting around in the seats, from side to side, passing my troops as we flanked the Carthaginian army. After all we had too be there at the frontlines when the brutal conflict begins. We had too, or the Carthaginians will be decimated.

The Romans are pursuing. Giving a full speed ahead chase of their adversaries. The two commanders advance their troops in a forced march. Plowing down the land with the spasmadic rhythm of the forward movement of their fast moving sandalled feet. That, accompanied with the clanging of their swords against their scutums and chainmail armor as they race after their foes created far more noise than needed too cover the engine of our little jeep as we race along the country-side.

The Carthaginian general set up his battle-lines where he thought he could use the hilly terrain too his advantage. In the mad flight the men got so disorganized that half of them were nowhere near their familiar spot in line. Since it was taking them so long too reorganize, a lot of the African soldiers were still not in the proper spot when the dreadful Romans came into sight. Unfortunately the Romans march in formation no matter what. Even a forced march. Hell, they even flee in formation. So needless too say the Romans were quickly ready for battle. By the time the two commanders gave the order for the charge to begin the Romans had shortened the distance and the Carthaginians were still frantically trying too get themselves together, however they had lost their composer long ago and their was no hope of retrieving it. The Romans are bolting forward. The clanging of their armor loudly jangleing as they race to assult their enemy. Frightened, the left side of the Carthaginian line foolishly stepped forward too meet the Roman threat, and in doing so, separating themselves from their brothers in arms. This allowed the Roman forces to completely encircle and route the Carthaginian flank. They now turn their gaze at the rest of the Carthaginian army, dashing forward to aid their Roman brothers who are currently cutting down their opposition.

This has too stop and it has too stop now! The thunderous signal is given and the troops move out. The signal this time is the emphatic echoing of the Gewehr ninty-eight that is being sported by our two platoons of sharp-shooter rifle troops who, perched a-top one of the many hills that dots the Metaurus battlefield are trying too pick off Roman Centurions, but not limiting themselves too just such targets.

The Gewehr ninty-eight is first manufactured in the year eighteen ninty-eight by the Mauser Rifle Company and will be standard issue for the German infantry until nineteen thirty-five. It is a one thousand two hundred fifty millimeters long, bolt action rifle that takes a five round clip of seven point ninety-two by fifty seven millimeter shells. The particular model we're carrying was not introduced until nineteen-fifteen when it was decided too fit a handful of Gewehr ninety-eights with telescopic sights for sniper usage. Though in order too do this the bolt had too be modified to a handle turned down position as opposed to a handle protruding out position. The telescopic sights consisted of models that magnified two and a-half times, or magnified three times. The deafening sound of the booming rifles repeating their vicious barks over and over, again and again was all our grenadiers, who were placed well ahead of the rest of our forces, needed to hear. That is their cue to start the assult. They charge downhill, steam-rolling ahead, in pursuit of the Roman legion that is in the act of preparing to out-flank the Carthaginian army, but they will not get the chance. The Romans, as of yet haven't realized that we are coming upon them, flanking their entire line from behind. The Roman legion crashes into the battle lines, aiding their Roman brothers, but they're not there for long when our grenadiers close the gap enough to let loose with their hybrid mixture of grenades. Our grenadiers are carrying a handful of different types of grenades. Yes, once again, they have with them the flaming ceramic jars of greek fire. They are also packing cast iron grenades. These are round, softball sized, hallow spheres with a wooden plug and fuse protruding from the top. They contain enough gunpowder too blow the casing into many unreconizable, fragmented pieces once the fuse was lit and allowed to snake it's way down toward the deadly powder. Also included in our arsenal of fun are glass bottle grenades. They, just like the cast iron grenades have a cork and fuse sticking out of the top and are filled with gunpowder. However, many of our glass bottle grenades also contain such things as b.b.'s, pebbles, and other surprises mixed into the gunpowder. I like too think of it as charity. I'm giving the Romans a little more bang for my buck. Free of charge. By far my favorite projectile tossing weapon is the infamous stinkpot. They are just glass bottle grenades but are filled with all kinds of foul, rancid stenches, that upon crashing into the enemy ranks cause those wretched Romans too double over and gasp in agony. These barbaric incindery devices upon hitting the ground and exploding, spew vomit, urine, human waste, burnt hair, rotting meat, rotting garbage, rotting flesh, dead animals, and whatever other nasty, rotten, offensive, stenchy smelling items we can think of. Roman soldiers are bending over and hurling, heaving their guts all over the ground while others frantically try too turn to run. The overpowering oder's dragging most of them down to the ground as they attempt to plow through their comrades to escape the explosive chaos that is taking place everywhere I look.

I am frozen in horror as I watch my Roman brother. His face imploding upon it's self. The dented helmet sailing off his head as though he were struck by a invisable spear that pierced his brain and was only forwarned by a strange sounding thunder that echoed from afar. Now what is this little ball that is rolling right toward me. As I ducked down behind my shield I abruptly found myself being pushed back with a strong velocity. The ear-splitting boom that proceeded the invisable shove that I felt left me swimming in a mental haze that only got worse when I tried too stand up. I never noticed the little metal slivers that were stuck in my scutum, just mere horsehairs from fully penetrating my shield and slicing my face into shredded meat. My buddies bodies, both with and without limbs are sailing all about me, landing with thuds that rebounded in my mind. I can't take it no more. I see a way out! can it really be? I step to runaway! As fast as I can but of course I don't get to far before I find myself gazing upon a strange beast of war. It looked like something that resembled a horse, but it's face was much different. Much more grotesque. What of the creature that was straddled upon him. It looked human. At least from the neck down. Who are these beings of war, beings of death and destruction. These must be Mars's Men.

Mars's Men. Yes, yet another name for Epitaph's Army Of Darkness.

The steeds we are riding are wildly powerful horses that have been herded up from the local Italian country-side. Since they have been roaming this landscape all their lives and are very familiar with the geography we decided that they are best fit too aid us on this mission. Ha! Ain't that funny. Italian horses being used to destroy Romans. Too make sure our forces don't become ill from the stinkpot bombardment that has just rained down upon those Roman scum both our cavalry and infantry troops are wearing gas masks similar too those of World War One. These are rubbery masks with built in plastic like lenses that have a hose leading from the mouth to a canister filter. These filters contain charcoal and other agents that neutralize chemicals of various different kinds, more than adequate for how we're using them here. The canister itself sits in a pouch like bag with a strap so that the whole thing can be flung over your back and conveniently out of the way. With just a few modifications we outfitted the masks too fit over the horses muzzles with the pouches just dangling from their necks and it gave them a horrific look when you gazed upon them.

Our cavalry is bolting toward the epicenter of violence. The riders bouncing in their saddles as the hoofs pound off of the hardened Earth. The thunderous rumble as the horses draw closer and closer, flanking the Roman forces as many of them cut to run. Where do they think they're going? This is like shooting ducks out of a pond as I point my pistol at fleeing Romans frantically running to where again? Oh yeah, over anybody they can. Even their own brothern. I'm pointing the Eighteen Seventy-Three Single Action Army Revolver also known as the peace-maker. It's a six shot fire arm with a fixed sight on the barrels end. I'm holding the one piece, walnut grip tightly as it sweats in my hands. It weighs thirty-seven ounces and the safety is a half-cocked hammer, but who uses that? I holster the eighteen inch as I grab for the next size down, still killing Romans as I race by in pursuit of the Roman cavalry. Don't worry, i'm not done picking off Roman infantry. As I gallop past the main theater of combat, bouncing on the stallion beneath me I trade my current pistol for the three inch snub-nose version of the peace-maker. Your probably curious as too how I can carry all these pistols. I have two sets of holsters, one around my waist as usual and the other across my stomach. The longest of the firearms, the eighteen inch barrel is holstered around my waist. As for the small, snub-nose peace-maker I am wearing a shoulder holster which provides far more comfort than having a third holster across my chest. Galloping past the mobocratic pandemonium I take a few more quick pop-shots at the frightened Roman infantry as I speed towards the fleeing Roman cavalry. A few of our own cavalry stay behind too help trap the now encircled Roman infantry, but right now our own infantry has closed the gap and is fiercely smashing into the Roman forces, or at least what's left of them. Now that our own infantry has arrived into the fray of battle our snipers halt their stealthy activity. We don't need them accidentally picking off our boys.

Our infantry is wearing chain-mail armor with underlaying padding which is very similar too what the Romans themselves are wearing. We also are wearing helmets that they recognize but instead of wearing sandals our infantry is wearing twentieth century combat boots, we also are sporting trousers with plate armor. Our shields are what twenty-first century tactical swat would be using if they were kicking your door in right now. Similar in shape and size too the Roman scutum but far more sturdier. Now our weapon of choice, believe it or not, the scimitar. The scimitar, originating somewhere out of south-west Asia, is a relatively long, light-weight sword that protrudes into a curved point at the end. They come in a handful of different varieties and will first see combat sometime in the ninth century A.D. We decided too go with the tulwar that comes from India because unlike some of the other versions it is very useful at both thrusting and slashing and has a disk shaped pommel too provide a secure grip. By now, as a result of the brutal efforts of both us and the Carthaginians most of the Romans lie on the bloody, flesh covered ground. Their putrid guts being soaked up by mother Earth.

As the conclussion of the battle was drawing near, Hannibal and myself, on horseback now having abandoned the puddle jumper, trotted into the thick of it all. Some of the Carthaginians knew something was unusal and fled like cowards, with the banging of grenades and the rising of stenchy clouds of smoke and other foreign forms of war, I guess I can't entirely blame them but they are suppose too be professional soldiers and professional soldiers do not run no matter what!Most of them stayed though and fought till the end, like true soldiers.

Things are relatively quite now with the exceptional scream of a stray Roman in need of being gutted like a game animal. I turn to Hannibal and ask him "Are you ready for that miracle?" "What, you mean the way your forces decimated these Roman scum is not it?" I couldn't help but chuckle at his reply. "No, it is not." Without Hannibal's knowledge, I had already sent a envoy to the Carthaginian general asking him to meet me for peace negotiations, therefore I knew my men would be escorting him here very soon. Upon his arrival I could tell that he too is a tall man, his dark skin glistening in the sunlight as the sweat rolled off of him. His stern brow could be seen from the distance that separated us. He didn't have to draw much closer before

Hannibal's jaw hit the ground. "What kind of devilry is this, this is impossible!" he practically yelled. "What, your not grateful?" I comically asked, but before the words were even out of my mouth Hannibal was already halfway across the field on his way towards the envoy. When he got there he swiftly dismounted the stallion he was upon and quickly embraced the Carthaginian general. Holding the big man at arms length away Hannibal started too touch and caress the Carthaginians face in both shock and disbelief. "Hasdrubal?" he asked. "I thought I would never see you again." "I'm on my way to join you, thank goodness your here. We must combine our forces if we are too defeat Rome or all is lost, they've captured all of New Carthage, we must stop them here!" was Hasdrubal's response. By now I've come upon the two of them and Hannibal fiercely turned to face me. "You've not answered me, how is this possible and what all does he know?" "He knows nothing of anything, and your not ready too know how I work such magic, however I promised you a miracle and I have delivered. Now, will you join me and Beelzebub's Boys in our war of righteousness. I promise, you'll get too kill many Romans." I said with a shining smile.

Now I know what some of you students of history are thinking. Caesarion, The Battle of the Metaurus didn't happen like that. How many times do I have too tell you, your looking at the wrong history book. You need a two thousand eighteen or newer, History of the World, Teacher's Annotated Edition. However if you were correct that might explain why Hannibal is still in shock. It was a warm night in two zero seven B.C. when his men brought him a package sent by the Romans. A package that contained the severed head of his brother, Hasdrubal. Until then, he never knew his brother was even in Italy and Hannibal remembers that night so clearly, so vividly, as if it were just last night. So for Hannibal to be standing here now, in front of his long dead brother Hasdrubal, everything to him is a hazy dream. time moving so slowly, as if everything is somehow surreal but not real, all at the same time. Of course Hasdrubal knows nothing of what his fate would have been had we not stepped in to intervene and Hannibal won't quit questioning me about it. He did reluctantly agree too fight the righteous fight and we brought Hasdrubal aboard as well. They are somewhere in sometime being trained and educated in the arts of modern warfare. Twenty-first century warfare. Oh, I'm sorry, I got side tracked again. I was suppose too tell you where we went after we left Boudicca.

The morning air is crisp with a slight, chilly breeze. The dew on the grassy ground as a result from the rain of the night before is causing the thick fog to rise through-out the hilly terrain. The already naturally poor visibility is even worse now in the wee hours of this wet and foggy June morning. Troops from the two opposing armies are practically across from each other and aren't even aware of it. Both of them set out early hoping too gain some kind of surprise or advantage over the other. The real surprise came however when, through the thick, dense fog they found themselves spying on each other. The shocked men on both sides quickly sprung into action. Violently hurling javelins and spears upon one-another in a desperate attempt to gain some kind of control of the spontaneous conflict they have found themselves engaged in. The two contenders in this combatative contest are first off, yep, you guessed it, Rome. This time they're being led to their doom by a chap named Titus Quinctius Flamininus. He's rather young for a consul but having seen battle action in the Second Punic War helped prop up his credentials as a capable commander. Rome was called upon for aid by a league of greek city-states, and since Titus could speak Greek very well and was a huge admirer of Greek culture he was perfect for this appointment. Upon his arrival he was hailed as both a hero and liberator. His portrait was emblazoned onto the side of coins. They treated him as though he were a living deity. He had been sent too help protect them from the Macedonian menace that had been boring down upon them since Rome's defeat at Cannae in two sixteen B.C.

Macedonia has been under the capable leadership of Philip the Fifth since two twenty-one B.C. He was a daring and courageous ruler who, like other great generals, liked to lead his men into battle from the front of the line himself.

When the skirmish between the two reconnaissance forces broke out the Romans were climbing out of one of the gullies that lays amongst the many hills that dot the countryside. By now reinforcements have arrived for both sides and the Battle of Cynoscephalae is on. It's one ninety-seven B.C. and the Macedonians hold the high ground. Back and forth the battle raged. The Romans charging up only to be pushed right back down. This tug-of-war, king of the mountain battle waged on for quite some time. Eventually Philip decided, against better judgement, that the time has come to take the initiative. Philip fought battles in the phalanx style of war which didn't suit the up and down hilly terrain that is Cynoscephalae, but he couldn't allow the Romans to strike first. He sent his men forward against the Roman legions. Upon contact the two armies were locked in a fierce face-to-face fight to the death. Everyone pushing and-a-shoving, a cutting and-a-gutting the enemy that stood before them, and even though the Romans were being slowly pushed down the hill, the battle was essentially one big stalemate. However those adept Romans thought they had found a way to win. Titus decided too pull out the big guns, or in this case the heavy beasts-of-war. During his time in the Second Punic War Titus learned a couple of tricks fighting against our comrade Hannible. One of those tricks was how too use elephants. He had brought twenty of them with him and now decided that in order too break the stalemate he would set them free against the Macedonian's left flank. So onward they come, charging head strong enroute to the left side of the frontline. Their large, floppy ears flapping in the breeze as these monstrous animals rush towards the Macedonian side of battle. Their proboscises sticking in the air, loudly blaring like organic trumpets. The landscape violently shaking as they charge forward. The trembling of the Earth as they get closer and closer. The quaking of the ground as they approach their intended victims. For as ear-splitting and deafening as the roaring, stampeding elephants are, they were nowhere near as load as the cacophonous boom of the firearms being toted by the Epitaph Elephant Extirpaters.

In the middle of The Great War, or what you think of as World War One, the German army was forced too deal with the new threat of mobile fortresses, too you that would be primitive tanks. Beginning in nineteen-sixteen both the French and British started too deploy these menacing machines of mayhem in a attempt too break the almost two year long standoff that had developed between the two opposing forces. This forced the Germans too come up with an effective counter-measure. Their solution, The Mauser Nineteen-Eighteen T-Gewehr. Yes, it took them two years too come up with this heavy calibre, high velocity rifle, but since it's sole purpose was too stop tanks, it will most definitely bring down a elephant. Manufactured by the Mauser company, this one hundred and sixty-nine centimeters long, bolt-action, single shot rifle shoots a thirteen point two millimeter cartridge and has a effective range of five hundred meters, but my troops won't be that far away. I only have fifteen of these particular units at my disposal which unfortunately ment that some of Titus's elephants were going to make it through and that also, unfortunately there will be Macedonian collateral damage, but hey, it's war, what can I say. Bad things happen. As the opposition elephants come barrelling onward, loudly announcing their arrival as they approach the frontlines, the Epitaph Anti-Elephant troops let loose with a thunderous volley from the T-Gewehr rifle. The Roman forces that are following behind their monstrous comrades don't hesitate, even at the sight of three-quaters of their elephants falling to the ground, to follow those few remaining that make it to and crash through the frontlines, violently steam-rolling right over those poor souls that were in the way. Knocking them to the ground before charging into the distance too no longer play a role in the battle before us.

Pandemonium has struck the Macedonian side of battle. Panic stricken soldiers throw their pikes and shields to the ground as they turn to flee. Chaos ensues as the Romans pursue their terrified foe. The relentless Romans don't have too pursue their enemy very far. The Macedonian phalanx is a very close and tight formation. Each man barely three feet from his warrior brother. So in their invain attempt to break and run they were frantically pushing and shoving each-other to the hardened ground. Unintentionally stomping and grinding the bodies of their Macedonian kin into the Earth. Forcing them too literally eat a face full of dirt before they die from the force blunt trama of being repeatedly stepped on and pulverized into the hilly terrain.

While this chaotic confusion is going down, Titus sees his opportunity to outflank what is left of the frontlines. To get behind and completely rout what is left of the Macedonian forces. Titus leads the charge himself, personally taking command of the reserve legions that are laying in wait. Little does he know I have a surprise for him. I brought my own big guns. I mean beasts-of-war. Titus had his elephant troops, so I brought my bovine battalions. Almost a quarter of my animal army consists of Texas Longhorn Cattle. These animals aren't wild beasts of nature. They are a blending of different cattle species and come in a variety of diverse colors. Their horns, from tip to tip can reach lengths, believe it or not, of almost seven feet. If your in any way familiar with cattle then you know these over grown critters are usually docile and gentle, but even the gentlest of beasts are quick too anger when you brand them with a red, hot, firey, poker. The remainding array of my bestial brood is the pride and joy of the bovine forces. With their aggressive tempers they put the real ter in terror, fear in fearful, the awe in awestruck. I can already picture the Romans shaking in their sandals before they cut and run. Cause this breed of cattle is huge, enormous, gargantuous. I'm talking about the bovinen monsters known as the Aurochs. I know you twenty-first centurions have no idea what i'm talking about because mankind, in his infinite wisdom hunted these animals into extinction long ago, but they were plentiful and abundant in my time. With their lyre shaped horns that point directly at you, they stand six and a-half feet tall and weigh almost twenty-two hundred pounds. I personally call them skunk cattle because they have a white stripe straight down their backs.

By now we've branded them with the pokers and they're rushing toward the frontlines. Churning up the grassy ground before stomping it into mud as they race closer and closer to the ensuing battle. The ground rumbling and shaking. Shaking and quaking more violently then a ten point zero earthquake rattling your backyard. Soldiers on both sides are attempting to flee, but it's too late. Large numbers of cattle crash into mobs of men as if they're living bulldozers, knocking them into the waiting arms of mother Earth. Those that are lucky are killed instantly. Many unfortunate men are laying on the ground with broken ribs and sternums gasping for breath while bleeding internally. Others screaming in agony with broken arms and legs that are shattered to bits as though they've been snapped like twigs. Their blood, bones, and sinew sticking out, exposed to the elements while dripping and oozing to the ground. Lets not forget those poor souls that recieved a free ride courtesy of being gored by the powerfully, forceful, strong horns of one of the many bulls.

Do remember too keep in mind that most of this frantic action is taking place towards the left side of the frontlines. However these frontlines are stretched out so long and wherever you happen too be at on them, the loud chaos is at such a frenzied high pitch that there is noway you would be aware of what is happening as little as five men away. So needless too say those poor chaps on the far right side have no idea that the left side has been completely decimated and has long since collapsed. This is however a good thing. It has effectively opened holes that allow the Epitaph infantry too utterly exploit.

As usual, The Epitaph infantry is wearing ballistic resistant jackets and although we are donning helmets, they are like nothing no Roman has seen before. If it wasn't for the seriousness of their current situation those foul smelling, scuzzy looking Romans would probably be laughing at us for wearing our grub dish on our heads.

The tin hat or Brodie helmet came into being by John L. Brodie in nineteen-fifteen as a direct result of The Great War. As a consequence of the introduction of gunpowder plate armor became obsolete and the militaries of the world failed too pursue protective gear of any kind for their soldiers. This really didn't matter for awhile as the first firearms were very inaccurate at best, however by the time the war had broke out handguns were almost the dead-aim, precision, bullseye hitting pieces you all rely on today. This caused many problems for soldiers on either side and as a result of the trench style warfare that had developed men on both sides were recieving huge amounts of lethal head wounds forcing nations too come up with modern like helmets, thus The British Brodie. It is a single piece helmet made from a relatively thick sheet of steel for added strength. The brim was about two inches wide. The helmet was also sporting a leather head-liner and chin strap. It was very efficient at providing protection from projectiles and shrapnel so long as they fell from above.

Engaged in battle I thrust my gladius at my enemy, pushing him back before angerly sticking him with the business end of my blade. But wait, who are these third party intruders.

The futuristic army that the Romans found themselves engaged against had successfully driven a wedge between them and their enemy.

We had approached from the flank, doing our best too position ourselves between the Romans and Macedonians.

Ha! Look at these idiots, they're pointing sticks at us. What are they thinking? This is gonna be like cutting fruit from a tree. So the silly Romans believed.

Now that the gap between us and the Romans is big enough we level our equalizers at the Roman riffraff. Firing off a volley of lead balls that are three-quarter of a inch in diameter. Lead balls that pierce right through the Roman scutum and penetrate deep into Roman flesh. The men on the Roman frontlines dropping harder than acorns on a fall, windy day. However, we are not going too take the time to reload the Brown Bess muskets we are carrying. We didn't want too give the Romans a chance to even contemplate about running away. Instead we are going too use the sixty-two inch long flintlock firearm to over-run the Romans with a all-out bayonet charge.

My feet pound off the hardened Earth as I bolt headstrong closing the distance between my adversary and myself. My heart pounding harder and harder as though it's going too burst straight through my chest. Sweat pouring down my brow, covering the rest of my body with the dirt and grime of the dust and crud of the days battle. The remaining Romans braced themselves for the inevitable crash that was about too happen. I smash into the frontline, heaving, pushing, and shoving the Roman before me. The stock of my weapon pointing to the sky. I thrust downward sticking my blade into the exposed top of my adversaries sandled foot. Feeling the blade of my bayonet piercing through the flesh and bones of my enemy's hoofs.

I hear a high pitched shriek only too discover it is myself. I reel back in pain as I stumble to the ground but before I even have a chance to fall I see the incoming wooden end of my enemy's boomstick as though this were all some kind of three dimensional fatal charade. I feel it's force as it smacks my face, busting my nose and splitting my lips. I see both my blood and helmet flying through the air as I continually desend down toward the ground. I feel wet chunks sliding down my throat, oh'wait, thats my teeth being escorted by some of my blood. I feel the thud ripple through my body as I finally hit the ground. I look up, expecting too see the beautiful blue sky but instead it is my unknown assailant with his magic boomstick standing directly over me. His shadow blocking the sun. Is this too be my last sight before I die. Now he's fixing to stab me with the bladed end of his noise-maker, at least i'm to numb too feel anything more, was the last thought of the doomed, unknown Roman soldier.

This scene was played out over and over, again and again until the Roman legions were utterly decimated. The Macedonians didn't know what too think of all this but they eagerly joined in the brutal fun.

The Brown Bess muskets we are carrying are capable of firing three to five rounds a minute, however you have too be pretty darn quick too accomplish this. Pouring the powder down the barrel then dropping in the lead balls. Ramming them home with the wooden ramrod, one of the last weapons too use them before iron rods were introduced. This all had too be done while standing up with the enemy shooting his own weapon at you. Talk about having to have nerves of steel.

The Brown Bess could be called the automatic rifle of it's day, not many weapons could shoot three to five rounds per minute no matter how skilled the operator. It weighed about fifteen pounds and had a effective range somewhere between fifty and one hundred yards. The bayonet was about eighteen inches long. Starting around seventeen twenty, this firearm will be standard issue to the British army for well over one hundred years. It will be the glue that holds the British empire together. The Brits' will use this gun too subjugate many parts of the world. Africa, India, Europe, North America. It's also the weapon that helped defeat Napoleon.

The name Brown Bess derives from the brownish color of the walnut stock. Also, what few weapons were mass produced in the early eighteenth century, most were coated with a brown like varnish on the exposed metal parts too act as a rust preventative.

Now that the Romans have been stopped at Cynoscephalae this will effectively put a halt to their eastward march. Had they been successful it would have opened the door for their brutal tyranny to overtake the entire middle east.

First we aided the Macedonians by setting up make shift field hospitals to assist the wounded. Of course we are using the latest in twenty-first century medical technology. Technology that they were of course awe-struck by. Also as usual we pulled out the propane barbecue grills and had a few nights of feastive celebrations.

Gaul. Summer of four fifty-one A.D. Atilla The Hun has been running roughshod all over the Western Roman Empire, sacking and destroying towns and cities at will. Cologne, Mainz, Triers, to name but just a few. However this is not just a senseless, barbaric assault all in the name of plunder and booty, no. Not this time! For this time Atilla is a husband who has been scorned. Just the year before the emperor Valentinian The Third had uncovered a mad, invain, plot by his own sister, Justa Grata Honoria too have him done away with so she could gain control of the throne. Valentinian had her taken away and incarcerated but not before she sent word to Atilla. She sent her royal ring and a braclet to prove her sincerity. She also offered her hand in marriage as well as co-ownership of the Western Roman Empire if he'll come to her rescue and dispose of her ineffectual brother.

So here we stand in a open field just somewhere outside Strasbourg, awaiting the Hunnic horde. What few Roman prisoners we took from previous engagements are lined up like the sacrificial lambs they are ment too be. However their is so few of them that we also have too forfeit up Epitaph Infantry Troops dressed as Romans as well. This is the sight that will behold the Huns when they arrive. A legion of what appears too be waiting Romans. Behind the fictitious band of Romans are old west style covered wagons and packed inside them is a little surprise. A device known as the Williams Machine Gun. First used in eighteen sixty-two as a secret weapon by the American Confederate forces, it has a four foot long barrel with a one point fifty-seven inch bore. Their is a hand crank on the right side that is turned clockwise and it fires sixty-five rounds per minute. It shoots good at a range of about two thousand yards until it overheats and then it has too cool down. About the only bummer of a drawback too this contraption of war.

I hear the thunderous hammering of the hoofs of the Hunnic horses as they pound off of the hardened Earth. I feel the vibration through the ground as they draw closer and closer. The uncontrolled perturbed emotions that arise with the anticipation of knowing that battle is near. The sweaty palms that make my weapon hard to hold. My heart pounding so hard it echoes within my ears but I am as ready as I am going too be.

It's the billowing cloud of dirty dust that's first visible before the barbaric horsemen appear atop their fierce steeds. They halt, wetting their lips at the sight of the human lamb-chops they intend to soon slaughter. The front Hunnic horsemen getting their bows to the ready position before they let loose with their miniature missiles that fly threw the sky like a swift bird with mighty wings, but instead of just passing by these birds dive to the ground, piercing the ranks of the artificial Roman front. It's a crying shame. I've just lost good Epitaph soldiers but, it's for the cause.

Some of my comrades around me drop to the ground, but we knew this was going too happen. I raise my shield and crouch to the Earth's floor as another wave of Hunnic arrows plunge down upon us. Before I stand the Hunnic horsemen are charging, their swords already drawn. They get pretty close but not close enough to see the scars that run down the left cheek that every male Hun recieves upon his entrance to this world before we let loose with the Williams Machine Guns.

The first few ranks of the Hunnic horde are cut too pieces. Hundreds of Hunnic men and horses lay slaughtered like swiss cheese on the now blood stained verdure. The rest of the barbarians turn too flee amid the chaotic, bewailing blare that loudly replies from the Williams Mechanical persuaders. He he, ha ha, lol. Those funny Huns actually thought they could cut and run. What were they thinking?

Our special operations troops, off-road division whip back the camoflage tarps they had concealed themselves with while laying in wait. As soon as they heard the bark of the Williams Machine Guns they knew too spring forth upon their motorized horses. At least thats what I'd think if I were a Hun. In all reality they are sitting upon the BMW R Seventy-Five. This is a German world-war two era motorcycle with a sidecar combination that will be produced from nineteen forty-one till the end of the war. It has twenty-six horsepower and weighs about nine hundred thirty pounds. This designed to go off-road bike has four gears, not counting reverse. It didn't take the bikers long at all to catch the Huns. Most of their horses, having never heard such a load, deafening, intense sound rear-up in absolute fear, dumbing their mounted riders to the ground before sprinting off. The men in the side-cars are having the time of their lives by pretending that they are the Grim Reaper. They're standing tall while firmly holding a scythe, a long handled sickle and slicing Huns in half while the motorcycle drivers wander around aimlessly at the next Hunnic target. Blood flying every which way while Hunnic torsos fall to Earth, leaving their bodyless legs too stand a few moments before they too flop down to the ground. This was continued until the Huns were completely decimated, including Attila. With phase one completed, before the Romans discover anything it is now time too march against the capital of Rome.

Ravenna: Capital Of Rome

It was a warm, breezy summer day when the barbarians arrived outside the gates. Thank God the city walls are both tall and thick. Rumor has it that it's Attila himself and that he will spare the city and everyone in it if the emperor Valentinian The Third abdicates the throne. However he won't. He seems too think we can hold out indefinitely, but I don't know. Has he thought about our food supply?

Under a banner of truce I sent Valentinian a ultimatum. Surrender or face the consequences. He, of course, choose the later. So hey, let the fun begin!

It was the third or fourth day they were camped outside the city when they started too wheel up the funny looking cylinder like tubes. It could have been comical, had it not been for the seriousness of the situation, but the calmness of me and the other residents soon turned too fear. Those funny looking cylinder tubes not only barked out a thunderous, ear-splitting boom but they also spit out good-sized round, metal balls that upon impact of the city walls took out huge chunks of concrete.

I had decided too siege the city and had the twenty-four pounders brought forward. They're only sixteenth century smooth bore cannons, but they'll do the trick. I'm hoping a few weeks of constant bombardment, day and night will get the emperor too reconsider.

How long can this madness go on? It's only been a few weeks and already I'm a nervous wreck. I'm not the only one, a lot of us city dwellers have had very little sleep lately, and my ears. Both my ears and my head have been constantly ringing for, I don't know how long now. If this don't stop soon, I myself will throw the emperor out to the Huns. Do I dare think, how much worse can this get?

I sent Valentinian another message today. My demands are the same, surrender or else. Already the city walls look like the cratered moons surface with all the holes and cracks and what have you not as a result of all the cannon balls that have been bouncing off of them these past few weeks. I guess it's time too step up the pain, I mean campaign.

We didn't realize at first, but after a few times we learned too hit the ground where-ever we where when we would hear the ker-plunk that preceded the firey explosions. It's as if little pieces of hell were being dropped down upon us. How is this possible? The Huns have found a way to throw some kind of magic weapon right over the walls and upon hitting whatever it explodes, causing everything around too be leveled to the ground. Entire homes and other buildings have collapsed as a result of this new Hunnic form of terror. And when these new Hunnic wonder weapons hit, they send debris and shrapnel flying everywhich way so you'r not safe where-ever you are. Things have gotten so bad I wish they would just hurry up and end this all.

Ravenna has been reduced down to a pile of rubble and ruin. Hardly anything stands erect anymore, there are shells and remanents of things that used to be buildings. I think. I've lost lots of good friends these last few days. As for myself, I'm more gone now than ever. The lucky ones are those of us who have died. I've not slept in who knows how long, I constantly have the shakes and my legs are so weak and wobbly I dare not try too walk to far. I don't know if it's from lack of sleep or lack of food. Probably both as food supplies are very low, after all the Huns have been terrorizing us for about two months now and they're still shooting the walls. Soon there will be a hole big enough for them too just walk right threw but hell, even if they got in today who can stop them? Those few of us that are left are so weak from starvation and sleep deprivation all the Huns would have too do is push us to the ground where we would be as helpless as a turtle on it's back. Not that that would stop them from killing us anyway. "Oh shit, here comes another one. Get down!"

I heard Cicerous yell "Get down!" but before I could even look in his direction his bodily fluids were raining down upon me as if he had exploded from the inside out. Bits of what I think are his brains and guts land all over me. Spatters of blood in varying sizes and designs also land all over me turning my bright, white tunic to a dull organic red. Sticky, slimy sinew lands on my face, head, and forearms, unfortunately some of it also lands in my open, gapping mouth leaving the nastyist of tastes you never want to know. I immediately hurl at just the thought of knowing that I just swallowed itty, bitty pieces of another human being. I turn once again in the direction he was standing but all that remains other than a giant rut, deep into the ground is patches of blood soaked grass and tiny pieces of shredded meat. shredded meat that used to be my friend. "Cicerous!"

The emperor's stubbornness has forced me too get a little more aggressive now. Hopefully this will learn him. I've dispatched about a company of troops to begin the terror campaign. They've been armed with the type eighty-nine grenade/mortar shell discharger also known as the knee mortar, but trust me on this if you do actually try to brace it on your knee and fire it you will greatly regret it. Don't believe me? go ahead, be a idiot and try it, but don't say I didn't warn you. This is a Japanese weapon that will see battle action from nineteen twenty-nine until the end of world war two. To use it the first thing you do is put the curved support plate on the ground. Not your knee, lmao! You then drop the two pound, fifty millimeter, light mortar round shell into the twenty-four inch long, rifled tube like barrel. You then fire this invention of war by pulling the handle like lanyard and sending the projectile flying towards it's target. It can fly about seven hundred and thirty-five yards but I've stationed my troops about one hundred and ten yards outside the city to ensure maximum destruction, ha ha. We've been dropping mortars on the city for a few weeks now and was fixing too send in another wave when white flags went up all along the wall. What was left of the city gates were swiftly flung open and the bound up emperor was forcibly shoved outside. The Roman messanger delivered the hand written note that read:

Dear Atilla,

Thank god you'r here. I apologize for all that you've had to endure and go through these last few months and that it took me so long to gather up those that are loyal to me but we had to ensure that the peoples support was behind me one hundred percent. Both the city and I are yours for the taking and I can't wait for you to take me all over the foyer floor. Soon I, and all of Western Rome will be your's to rule as you see fit. Here is my insipient fool of a brother who, for years tried to be just half the ruler you are and of course he couldn't even stand in your shadow. See you soon!
- Princess Honoria

Finally! Rome is mine. Well, at least the western half. If only they knew just who I really am, but before I lead them to their doom, I will embrace them to my bosom.

I have too put on the appearance that I'am going too be a righteous ruler and my first act is to send word to every town and settlement between Rome and Ravenna that I, their new Caesar, is moving the capital back to Rome, where it belongs, ha ha. Really I just want what should've been mine a long time ago. A victory parade through the streets of Rome.

Rome: Four fifty-one A.D.

For the first time in decades the streets of Rome are alive with the sounds of festive celebrations. Song and dance fill the air as the people are giddy and gay with excitement and anticipation. Vendors line up and down almost every street trying too sell their product of choice. Commoners have travelled from all over the peninsula to see the Caesar who returned the capital of the empire to it's namesake city. And what a perfect day it is for such a event. It's a beautiful summer day. Even though the sun is shining it's not so hot that you sweat buckets just standing still. That's probably something too do with the nice, cool breeze blowing ever so gently through-out the city.

Trumpets blare, signaling that the beginning of the royal procession is approaching and the exciting cheers of the peolpe loudly ring out, proclaiming their joy that Rome is once again the seat of power.

The first thing the bunched-up, standing elbow to elbow crowd experiences is the beautiful vestal virgins, in their pure white, almost see through garments paving the way for all that is to follow by tossing red and purple roses up into the air. The roses slowly float back down to Earth and moments from now will be trampled to smithereens by not only other humans but animals as well. Immediately following the virgins are other maidens and male servents who please the crowd by tossing grub of all kinds in their direction. Mainly bread and bread products such as muffins and biscuits and no, not the muffins and biscuits that adorn the plates of you twenty-first centurions. The crowd also recieves other goodies as well, such as cheese, sausage, pastries, fruits and nuts of all kinds. I even bestowed exotic delicacies upon the people such as cocoa, chocolate, coconuts, corn and other new world goodies. Immediately afterward to proceed me in my miles long parade is a pair of beautiful, magnificently, alluring looking wolves. Predominately gray in color, but under the sun in the correct angle, they have touches of red and other colors, almost like a calico cat. The wolves, just like every other animal to follow in my entourage outside their beauty also have a symbolic meaning and these particular wolves symbolize the rebirth of Rome. The first wolf stands for the original birth of Rome and the second for it's rebirth which is happening now, under my direction and control. Next in line is a ram with it's mighty horns to demonstrate my authority and leadership. Third is a volture with it's brightly colored head and deep, dark, black feathers. Some ancient, now insignificant religions believe the volture too be a mysterious creature that comes and goes at will, almost as if in to thin air. So this exact one that is now before the euphoric crowd symbolizes my spontanoues conception, or what appears too be a spontanoues conception, thanks too Epitaph's time machine, people will think for centuries I come and go at will, into thin air. Thank-you Lord Epitaph! Next is the mighty lion, which symbolizes my strength and fearless courage. Fifth is a tribe of wild boars too represent my fierceness in combat and my willingness too fight to the death. He, he, ha, ha, my enemies death. To follow them is a potent, stout, asian tiger for my power and energy. Now you might be surprised at my next choice. The little tortoise, but he's here for my invulnerability too attack. Attack of any kind. It's nice too have a protective shell covering my backside. To follow him is the quilled porcupine. He's here for my protection. Next is a duck-like pelican to symbolize my self-sacrificing charity and devotion too those who are willing to follow and fight for Epitaph! Last, but by far not least is a herd of bulls. Some of them fresh off of the Cynoscephalae campaign. Not only do these giant beasts exemplify my potency and fertility but following the bulls were more bulls, pulling long, flat carts and upon these carts, too once again personify my manhood sat huge, wooden phalluses, and yes ladies, I really am that endowed.

We're not at a end yet. The celebration continues with a astonishing display of Roman deities. Roman deities that appear almost life like. Carved out of wood and standing about six feet tall, they appeared even bigger due to the fact that, just like my phalluses, they are being towed on carts by large size bulls. The Aurochs.

The first demigod to greet the gleeful Roman crowds is Amor, the playful Cupid who, if animate, would glid through the air with his angelic wings and his little thing just dangling in the breeze for all too see. After all, he did like to roam around naked for some reason. He always carries a bow and quiver of arrows. Some tipped in gold, others in red and when he shots you with one your affection for others would increase greatly. Just like the animals, all the deities in my procession have a symbolic reason for being here and cupid represents my undying love and commitment to Epitaph's people. Following Cupid is Fortuna. She, like most females is a mysterious being who wears a dark veil over her face. She has small, stubby wings that protrude from her backside and in one of her hands she carries a cornucopia or horn of plenty. It is overflowing with all kinds of goodies, food, flowers, grain, candy, anything you can imagine. Legend says the horn comes from a goat that nursed off of Zeus but, hey, whatever. She's here as the goddess of good luck and fortune for all those that believe onto Epitaph! Directly behind her is yet another female idol. Ceres. She's more of what you would call a tom-boy. She ain't afraid too get down and dirty for a hard days worth of honest, hard work. Sometimes she carries a highly decorated scepter or staff with beads, feathers, and other trinkets dangling from it. She carries a basket of fruit, flowers, and other such earthly goods. From time to time she will enhance her looks by adorning her head with a garland of corn and for clothes she covers herself in nothing but fig leaves. You know, the kind used by Adam and Eve after they discovered their shame. As you may have noticed, everything Ceres does or has is in one way or another connected to nature which is why she is here. As the goddess of agriculture she shows how over abundantly those loyalist to Epitaph are taken care of in all that is physically needed such as food, clothes, shoes, etc. Coming in fourth is Neptune, god of the sea. He's not seen by humans too often as he is usually cruising the ocean floor when not residing in one of his many underwater castle like dwellings. He has shoulder length, dark, curly hair and often carries a pitchfork looking trident with him. He also sometimes wears a coral crown around his head which kind-of highlights the full beard that is firmly strapped to his face, and the robes he wears seem to stick like puddy to his muscular torso. He's here so that Epitaph naval troops have good tidings while at sea. After all, too anger this deity could bring about much disdain because with no effort at all he can easily summon up both tsunamis and tidal waves. Next is Vulcan, the god of fire. I almost feel sorry for him as he had a very rough start in his life as a deity. Because he was born with a dark, grotesque looking reddish, tinted skin his mother saw fit to discard him by violently throwing him off of the tallest mountain she could find. He now wears nothing but bright red tunics and uses a cane as one leg is now shorter than the other as a result of that fatal event upon his entry to life. His birth mother would eventually regret tossing him to his fate when she learned that he became a pretty clever and crafty blacksmith. He could hammer almost anything into exsistance once he put his mind too it and it's not uncommon at all too see him carrying a set of tongs or a hammer or any other smithing tool for that matter. However he is being paid hommage here today as we need fire too burn with us. Not against us. Sixth is Pluto, god of the underworld. His eyes are like blood red rubies that glisten in the darkness of hell and he proudly sits upon a pitch black horse. A horse that is as black as night. Off to one side of him is his pet, the three headed dog, Cerberus. Cerberus guards the entrances of the underworld for Pluto so that those who are trapped inside, never get out. He has a tail like a snake and upon his head is a mane of live snakes, just like the one Medusa has. Pluto symbolizes the death and destruction that will befall all those who oppose Epitaph. Next is Mars, the god of war. He stands before the Romans now donning everything a Roman soldier would be accustomed too wearing. A crested helmet, full body armor, shield, sandals, and a sword which he is proudly protruding above his head in a defiant gesture too anyone and everyone. Mars embodies my prowess in war. To follow him is the last of the female deities. Juno, queen of the gods. What can I say, she's the queen. You have to keep her happy. Next is Jupiter, king of the gods. You have to pay hommage to the king or all will be against you. Both the king and queen are decked out in robes and sandals. They both wear diadems around their heads. Juno holds a staff while Jupiter holds a spear. Perched on his right, outstretched hand is a mighty eagle. The loudly, cheering crowds were shocked silent as they gazed upon this last deity. They couldn't seem too recollect who this one is. Soon no Roman, or anyone else for that matter will ever question who this God is. Towering over the other deities at a little more than twice their height, this made of granite, finely polished, just a tad over twelve feet tall statue reveals very little of the being it represents. He wears a robe, like one a medeval monk would have, that hangs all the way to the ground. It's pulled so far over his head that his facial features are completely obscured in everyway possible. Outside of the tips of his combat boots that just extend a wee little bit outside of the overflowing robe, all that is visible is his hands. In his left, clutched ever so closely to his torso is somekind of sacred book, what, I'm not quite sure. Now in his right hand, that is proudly held above his head is a little square device with a circle in the center. I've asked him many times what this is and the only answer he gives me is "It's the button, and be happy I ain't used it. Yet." Yes. This deity is the Epitaph himself. The only deity that is truely alive! Following Epitaph is the reason the Romans are here. Thats right, Me! I stand firmly on my float wearing a diamond studded diadem of my own. I boastfully exhibit my finest purple linens to display my claim to royalty. I carry a staff in one hand, a spear in the other. I too am wearing modern boots. I egotistically hold my posture as we passby the once again screaming crowds. I'm not on my cart alone. Along with my new Roman queen, Honoria I am once again surrounded by maidens and servents. They toss out more food to the enchanted Romans as well as the new Roman currency. Gold and silver coins. These ain't just any coins, no! Emblazoned on one side is a portrait of yours truely, on the other is a silhouette of Lord Epitaph. Years from now, in the youthful days of your great-grandchildren, not only will these coins once again be the monetary system of Rome, but they will be the currency of the world!

Part II

Awareness

It's a crisp, fall day with a mist of heavy fog surrounding the peaks of the hazy, blue mountains that lay in the distance. It matters not if you walk or drive the narrow, one lane path for either way you will witness the same awe inspiring, breath taking, spectacular sights. Here you feel as if you are one with nature. Wide open fields that are probably bursting with overgrown foliage in the summer but are now withering away, awaiting for the cold, sickly hand of winter too snuff them out of life. The trees in some spots shroud the roads from the elements of mother-nature as if they are organic tunnels. In some spots the floor of the cove is covered in leaves of various colors. Mostly dull red and burnt brown. However their are many trees that still have their leaves clinging percariously to them, like a tic on a dog. Mainly the decrepit, brown, dead ones that refuse too let go of life, but their are others as well. You have red in a variety of different shades, maroon being one of them. Many leaves are two-toned. Their's lilac purple and sunshine yellow as well as greenish yellow, but my favorite leaves are the ones that proudly fall to the ground in volunteer orange with Tennessee pride.

These are just some of the breath-taking wonders you will witness as you travel along The Cades Cove Loop Road. Cades Cove is just a little section in the south-western half of The Great Smoky Mountains National Park located in eastern Tennessee. The Cades Cove Loop itself is a eleven mile circle that takes you past many historic sites such as cabins and churches as well as log homes. One of the more memorial sights is the Primitive Baptist Church that was built in eighteen eighty-seven. It miraculously stands on bronzish, orange stones. As many as three high in some places. It also has six windows, three on each side and dual doorways that beckon you to come on in, except when your there the doors are long since gone and discarded. Just in back of the old church sits a tiny cemetery, the oldest of headstones being from the late eighteen hundreds.

Every year, millions of people visit this place without ever having a clue as too what they're walking and driving over, everyday. For deep within the ground, a few miles down sits a top secret, black operations, underground government bunker. So top secret that very few of the Cades Cove employees even know of it's exsistance. It's only accessible by wandering off of a few of the many hiking trails that criss-cross the cove. As for the individuals that actually work down there, they are holed up inside for months at a time. Sometimes even longer.

We were sent by the higher-ups to retrieve files, paperwork, and computer data about the on-goings of a location within someplace known as Cades Cove. I was very excited about the opportunity as this was my first real in the field assignment since joining the C.I.A. As usual, we weren't told much. Only that it at one time had been used for conducting top secret work and that the facility had been abounded, but it was going too get me out of both, the office and D.C. I will be under the supervision of my immediate superior but that was okay. He's a easy going, laid back kinda guy thats not hard too get along with in anyway. He is caucasian and about mid-fortyish. He either dyes his jet-black hair or hides the gray very well, I don't know which. His name is Donald Darby and we've worked together the entire nine months I've been assigned to the department. I myself being a oriental girl, around five foot three, consider myself kinda plain to look at. After all, us orient's are about the same. Copper skin. Deep, dark, brownish, blackish eyes. Jet black hair in various lengths. What else is their too say of us. My name is Ylene Reyes, but you can just call me Lene. It's me and Don that are in charge of this operation but we were assigned three members of the National Guard too help us clear the goods out of this bunker like stronghold.

First there is Lashawn Shell. A very dark, tall, black man, who stands just a tad over six feet. He's been in The Guard about three years now and loves every moment of it. The next fellow with us is a chap named, and I still can't believe this, William Williams. What were his parents thinking? Needless to say he answers to nothing but Billy. Go ahead, call him William. He tends too get a little angry. He's a slender white man, about five foot eight, weighing, I would guess about one hundred thirty pounds with light brown hair and thin glasses on his face. Last is a North American native by the name of John(Running Dog)Baxter. I'm not sure just what tribe or breed he's from but he himself is around six feet with long black hair and steely cold eyes. He has a thin, cut tone with a presence that just screams "Leave me alone or I'll gut you from ear to ear." He doesn't say much and I leave him alone. All three of them are somewhere between the ages of eighteen and twenty-five.

When the facility was operational you had too enter through the north side. If you approached from any other direction the guards would instantly know that you didn't belong and you would never be seen again. People would assume, even the Cades Cove employees, that you just got lost in the mountains or eaten by a bear or mountain lion or something. There is only the two ways in or out. The north side door and the south side which was ment to be a emergency exit only. Both doors are very thick, solid pieces of reinforced steel that required swipe card identification while simultaneously laying your index finger inside a DNA identification slot as well as a retinal scan. You think that would be enough but in the days of full operation, as soon as you got through the door you would encounter very well armed guards who would still check your i.d. As soon as the guards approved your presence, you would be allowed to proceed but access would be limited depending on your clearance level. Very few were allowed to freely roam around the complex. Shortly past the guards you would come to a four-way. If you went right, to your immediate right would be the shower rooms. First the mens then the womens. Directly across from them is the bathrooms. Past all this the hallway deadends and you have to go left. Not to far up this hallway is the entrance to one of the generator rooms. Now if you go left instead of right you'll have the sleeping quarters directly to your left, first women, then men. Across from the bedrooms is a decent size kitchen/dining room. It has all the conveniences you could possibly think of. Stove, oven, microwave, everything, and it's stocked to the max with all kinds of foods. There's even a dining table so the personal don't have to eat in their bedrooms. Instead of going left or right you can choose to just go straight forward, which will take you right between the bathrooms and kitchen area to the next hallway. At this point, directly across from you is the recreational room. There is three ways in and out of this room. It is full of all kinds of stuff to help the employees forget about their work and environment for awhile, cause once your down here you are not allowed to leave for who knows how long. In the rec. room there's many t.v. sets with x-box, playstation and every other gaming system known to man. A huge selection of blue-ray movies. Fuzball table, ping pong table, computers. Straight forward and to your right are doors that lead out into hallways. To your left is the security guards office, and noone gets in except for security personnel. Behind the guards office is the filing room, nothing here but LOTS of filing cabinets. We have been ordered to get EVERYTHING out of this room. It doesn't matter if it's a piece of scrap paper laying on the ground. EVERYTHING must go! The security office has access to each hallway on either side, the left and right. The filing room behind it, and the recreation room in front of it. The guards needed instant access to every direction incase of a emergency situation. Upon entering the rec. room if you were to exit the doorway straight across from you, you'll find yourself in another hallway being, once again, confronted by guards. You need a higher level of clearance to be in this area. Once again you will need a swipe card i.d. to enter the room these guards are posted at. This is the research lab, another place we need too empty. Once again, everything in this room must go. If you go right the hallway will eventually t-off but will also take you past everything you've already been through. To your immediate left the hallway will end, forcing you to take another left. Back in front of the research lab if you go left this hallway will just dead-end, but not before forcing you to hang a right. Down this hallway is yet more guards. Once again you need swipe card i.d.'s to get into the room on the left. The walls of this particular room are very reinforced. Sound proof, explosion resistant, you name it. This is the experimentation room and just what they did in here, i'm not quite sure, however we've been ordered to poke around in here as well and to grab anything that looks like it's of interest. Okay! Thats a vague description. Almost everything in this whole building looks of interest. Makes me wonder what really went on here, but orders are orders and we do have a job to do. Straight past the experimentation room, to the right is yet another generator room. The generators are run by hydro-power. Some of the coves streams were sutely diverted and run underground where they would enter the generator rooms in one side and exit out the other, producing enough power for the entire facility.

It took us almost two weeks too get all these computers and other forms of documentation out of here. Considering this is the computer age I can't believe how many filing cabinets there are with actual handtyped documents. We grabbed all kinds of do-dads, gizmos, and thingy-ma-bobs other than paper documents from the research lab and experimentation room. Half these things I have no-idea what they are.

We took the back way out of the cove. Don was the one driving so I wasn't going too argue. We went out the Parson Branch Road and tried to traverse the tail of the mighty dragon. The dragon, route one twenty-nine, has more twists, turns, curves, loops, arches, bends, and bulges than you can shake a stick at. There's so many curves you'll be dizzy just half-way through. You'll think your on a roller-coaster. There's a little over three hundred turns in just a little under eleven miles, but I did see one funny thing that struck me as odd. A mesh, netted covered mountain. Whats the purpose of this? Did they think this small part of the Smokies is going too sprout legs and walk away?

As odd as that maybe the truely wierd stuff didn't start until we got back to D.C. Very few people in our department recognized Don and me, and those few that did wondered what we were doing there. They tried convincing me that i'm suppose too be in a different department clear on the other side of the building and that Don had been transfered out of here long ago, which was news to him. Things only got stranger. People we had been working with since I started were no longer there, and there was lots of faces that I know I had never seen before. Me and Don had taken it upon ourselfs, besides, who were we suppose to report to anyhow since no-one was who we remember them being, too track down those three guardsmen that had been with us at Cades Cove, maybe they know something we don't. How did things change so drastically? So quickly? We were only gone about two weeks! As far as I know, they were all stationed somewhere different, but luckily I remembered Billy saying that he himself had been posted at Camp Atterbury in Indiana. It might not be much, but it's a place to start.

Part III

The Byzantines

Well welcome back! For a minute there I thought you had left me. Where did you go? Snack break? Are you ready too continue? Now that Western Europe and parts of North Africa are firmly under Epitaph control it is time too turn our attention east toward those Byzantine Bastards the Eastern Romans. Flavius Petrus Sabbatius Justinious or simply Justinian The First was in his mid-forties when he ascended to the throne in five twenty-seven A.D., and he ruled for almost as long before kicking the bucket in five sixty-five. Though he rewrote the laws on the books and went on a massive building spree, that was financed by a huge boost in taxation, he was also a harsh, brutal tyrant who probably would not rate very well on a popularity poll. His laws are stern and anyone who in anyway opposed was promptly put to the sword. However this is not how he wanted his legacy to be remembered. He was hell-bent on being known as the emperor who reclaimed the boundries and borders of the original Roman Empire and just six years after taking power he set about this task. Starting in five thirty-three he set off on a number of non-stop, continuous campaigns to reclaim the lost Roman territories. He first aimed his sights at Hannibal's homeland Carthage, which Justinian believed too be under the control of Vandal barbarians who had been allowed too reside in the region but SURPRISE!! Thats right, this is all terrain of the budding Epitaph Empire. To lure the Eastern Romans into a false sense of security we put up a credible looking token resistance but pretty much let them have parts of North Africa as well as Sicily and Sardinia knowing that it wouldn't be long before we took them back, after all, we had to make him feel confident and cocky, right?

Justinian is now eye-balling what he thinks will soon be his main prize and it's shining like a glowing gem in the visions of his mind. This want-to-be prize is Rome and the rest of the Italian peninsula itself. In five fifty-two the emperor decides too make a play for the final jewel in his proverbial crown.

He sends a fleet across the Adriatic Sea that makes land near the town of Ancona. From here his troops, under the direction of one of his main commanders Narses, intend to make their way to the Via Flaminia Highway and just bulldoze their way the few hundred miles to Rome. They're so reassured of victory that they have already taken to calling the roadway The Byzantine Corridor. Well this is where they're fun stops, and our's starts.

In their minds it may be just a mere few hundred miles to Rome but the Via Flaminia not only cuts through towns it also cuts through woods, forest, mountains, over rivers, beside rivers, around rivers, basically it's more wild wilderness than civilized cities.

Around four-ninty The Ostrogoths, a homeless germanic tribe was granted permission by Epitaph negotiators to reside within the peninsula, however if threatened they would have too "Hold the fort." so too speak until Beelzebub's Boys could arrive. As soon as the goths became aware that the Eastern Romans were marching inland they sprang into action and rather than ambush the Romans at any one of the many feasible locations along the Via Flaminia they encountered The Byzantines in a flat, plain, field, that had very few hills surrounding it, outside the modern town of Gualdo Tadino at a place that shall be known as The Battle Of Taginae.

I can't help but notice how many of them there are and how few of us there is. There must be fifty-thousand plus Romans over there and our chief, Totila seems too think we can handle them. That we don't have too wait for our protectorates, the fearless Army Of Darkness, Tyr's Tormentors. I suppose he has good reason to think this, after all The Byzantines have been chipping away at the mainland for years now and so far it's been us who have had the task of trying to stop them without a sign or hint from the Epitaph Army but somehow this feels different, peculiar.

Upon viewing the massive accumulation of Roman forces Totila has decided that in order too buy time he must stall time and calls for immediate negotiations. He's hoping that this will give us time too formulate an effective battle plan against those abhorrent Eastern Romans, but the ruse didn't work. Their crafty commander, Narses somehow saw through our trickery as if he were gazing into somekind of mystical sphere or crystal ball. Next Totila requests that a duel take place. A single combatant of ours against a single combatant of theirs. He figured once again, that while these two men are skirmishing with one-another that maybe, just maybe the rest of us could concoct some kind of attack plan. Something. Anything!

Surprisingly The Byzantines actually agreed too this, so we sent forth one of our biggest warriors. He is armed like most other sixth century soldiers. He's equipped with a typical sword and a little round shield, unlike that tall vertical thing those wanna-be Romans use. His helmet not only has the built in neck guard in the back but also has hinge like cheek protectors that just flop down over the sides of one's face. Men on both sides still mainly wear sandals. The most important thing any warrior would be wearing is his gambeson or under-padding. These particular ones we have are stuffed with waded up horsehair but they could be made of wool, linen, cotton, and other such fabrics. Without your padding the hauberk, or chainmail armor that is covering you're frame would be pretty useless. Now I know what you're thinking, why are you still wearing chainmail when they invented Lorica Segmentata or plate mail, centuries ago. The truth is that first, it's just too hard to make. Secondly, it costs way too much money and us Ostrogoths are mainly farmers. Third, after the fall of Western Rome to the Epitaph Army the only nation left with both the funds and resources to produce it is our enemy on the other side of the field and even they don't make it in the numbers that Western Rome did. So other than us being outnumbered it's a fair fight. Yes Totila has plate mail as well as some of the other commanders but almost everyone else is wearing their mail.

The two verbally belligerent adversaries immediately went at it. Their swords and shields clanging and banging as they violently smacked off of the others. The two sporadically careened around one another. Ducking and weaving, weaving and ducking, almost as if they were engaged in somekind of strange dance, desperately trying too avoid the thrusts of his enemy's sharp, jaggedy weapon. The dirt and dust, swirling heavily around the two combatants as if a small tornado is hanging in the atmosphere of their immediate vicinity. They parry back and forth, left and right, zig zagging in no definitive pattern, each of them trying too pull every corrupt, low-down, sneaky trick they know in order too gain somekind of upper-hand, but all is fair in war is it not. Unless my eyes deceive me I don't happen too see anyone out there in striped tee-shirts reciting somekind of unknown rule book. Each fought fanatically for his respective faction. Neither one wanting to bring dishonor to their people by dropping the ball so to speak, or in this case the sword. However their could be only one victor and unfortunately it was not our agent that prevailed. I so hope that this is not a sign of things to come.

Though our man fell to that Roman scumbag on the other side his sacrifice was not invain. We scouted their frontlines and found a weak point. Before the lone Roman warrior was even half-way back to his camp the order was given for our cavalry too attack and engage. The Roman left flank was established at one of the few small hills that seperated us from them. When our horse-force breaks threw, breaching and penetrating the enemy lines, the infantry will be able too close the deal by outflanking The Eastern Romans. Completely routing them from behind.

Even though the Byzantine cavalry is smaller than our own, they were swiftly able too react to our oncoming assault and add the much needed support to their own infantry. They also mobilized a portion of their reserve troops quickly shifting them left. Even though by now the phalanx is a very outdated form of warfare those troops that were originally stationed on the Roman left flank were ordered into it anyhow while the emergency reserve forces will be both added support and plug-up any developing holes and cracks as a result of our live, motile forces. As outdated as the phalanx may be it does have one thing going for it, the protracted pikes it's frontline soldiers yielded.

These particular ones are almost eighteen feet long and as our horsemen galloped in toward those Byzantine Bastards they knelt down on one knee, holding their pikes with both hands while thrusting them upwards, stabbing our animal forces in their chests causing the horses to violently crash to the ground, throwing their human occupants threw the air like organic missiles right into The Eastern Roman lines only for them too be cut down by merciless enemy swords.

I can hear the horses neighing from here and there's a bit of a distance between us and them. I can't believe the horror I'm witnessing. How could this happen? Our cavalry should have been able too plow right threw them like a knife threw butter. This is completely unbelievable. Thank goodness our infantry wasn't ordered to follow our cavalry or me and all my comrades would be fixing too get cut to pieces right now. Oh no! What the? Oh my gosh! Now their cavalry has riden out from behind their frontlines and is smashing into whats left of our cavalry and their infantry has already gotten to it's feet, brutally cutting our men and horses to shreds. I guess this means Uluric's death by duel was invain.

Totila had too sound the retreat, but it's not like many made it back. He ordered us all to get in battle formations, but why? Their infantry outnumbered us almost three to one, and we no-longer had any cavalry so what is the point in this? What is he thinking? We should just break and run, live too fight another day. He said he would be back and that we better be ready for action.

It was just a few moments later that my jaw hit the ground and my eyeballs popped out of my head. Again! I don't believe what i'm witnessing. Our leader, Totila, donning his plate mail armor, that at the correct angle shines like golden bronze in the sunlight. His crested helmet, firmly planted upon his head had a vertical line of feathers all in a neat row that stretched to the back of his neck. Mounted on his overgrown stallion has marched out to the halfway point between the two armies, plainly visible for all too see. At first I thought that perhaps he was going too taunt or tease the enemy into battle so that just maybe they would make a mistake that we could capitalize on, but no. He strutted out at a moderate gallop but abruptly him and his steed started to whirl and twirl as if they were a animated merry-go-round. At the same time he was tossing around two tiny daggers as you would juggle tennis balls. His horse, while neighing, pranced and paraded. In almost timed intervals it would rear up on it's hind legs, frantically appearing too kick about it's front two airborne feet. Once back on the ground it would walk in reverse, going backwards. By now Totila had replaced the daggers with his full sized sword and was tossing it into the air by the hilt and catching it by the blade into the palm of his hand. What does he think this is? A carnival! What's next? Oversized clowns popping out of undersized, matchbox looking volkswagons. After about fifteen minutes of this he finally came bouncing back toward us.

It takes everything I have not too bust out laughing but I can't help but chuckle inside. I can't be the only one who is giggling too himself. I mean after all, come on. It looks like even our commander is wanting too roar hysterically but he is doing a admirable job at maintaining his professional dignity. I've met some dense people before. Both fellow Romans and others, but one of those brainless barbarians just trotted himself halfway over here and put on a circus show like I've never seen before. Hopping and dancing in circles of all sizes. Both beast and rider shuffling their feet to some unheard musical beat. And what of the rider. Sure, he's dressed in his best, but he's also playing a dangerous game of Russian roulette with himself by rhythmically tossing his sword and daggers into the air and then grasping them into his bare hands as they desend back down to Earth. It's only a matter of time till he sticks himself in the hand with one of those weapons of his then I will laugh, uncontrollably. I must say though, he's kind of entertaining. He would make a very good court jester back in Constantinople. The emperor would love him. If he wasn't a barbarian. He's made his way back to his camp though so I guess... Oh shit! Here they come!

Totila has us charging the Byzantine Roman frontline. He wasn't even completely back into camp yet when he gave the order. He must think his little sideshow has them caught off-gaurd. That's hope he's correct cause if not we're doomed.

Most of us don't even make it to the Roman frontlines which are set-up in a cresent shape form with the Byzantine allies front and center. They must thoroughly trust their allies who are also set-up in phalanx pattern. On both sides, and just a few steps back are the true blooded Byzantine Roman soldiers set-up in traditional Roman legion style. Beside them, once again a few steps back are the Byzantine archers. They are the very reason that few of us actually made it to the Roman frontlines. They had five thousand archers on both sides of their line. As soon as we were close enough that is ten-thousand little missiles raining down upon us. And they could reload very quickly. As soon as the first wave of arrows hit the next barrage was already in the air, fixing to puncture and pierce the chainmailed bodies of my comrade brothers. Everyone around me is dropping to the ground like flies. I'm surprised I'm still here to tell you this story, but not for long. I'm turning and fleeing, Totila can fight this battle on his own, I've had enough. Besides, the Byzantine cavalry is starting to pour around the infantry flanks, running our men down before slicing them to pieces. Or whats left of them. Also, The Roman army is now steadily advancing toward us. I'm sure Narses can taste victory. It's probably only a matter of time till he sends his forces toward us at a marching pace. After all, the only thing stopping him from finishing us off is air and opportunity. Oh geez. Guess I shouldn't have spoken, here they come. But wait. What do I hear? Those strange noises coming from behind me. Why, it's the euphoric cheers of my fellow Ostrogoths. What do they possibly have too cheer about? As I turn around to see what the commotion is all about I can't believe what my eyes behold. A giant swarm of troops rushing right at me. Oh my gosh, Beelzebub's Boys. It's about time!

Leading the charge into battle is the Epitaph Grenadiers. Yes, once again they're tossing every grenade known too mankind. Even the Byzantine ceramic jars of greek fire, which I find hilarious. Using their own weapon against them. A weapon they won't even invent yet for another couple hundred years. I know, I'm a pyromaniac. I just like watching things burn, especially Romans! He, he. The thunderous noise of the exploding grenades is causing the Roman horses to violently turn back. In the process, some of them tossing their human riders to the ground with a resounding thud. A thud that echoes throughout the ears and body of that particular Roman as he hits the firm, rigid terrain.

It's at this moment that our own cavalry is sweeping into battle from every direction with their sabres wildly flailing above their heads. The sabres, unlike a sword are curved at the end and have single-edged blades. Also unlike swords they have large hand guards that cover the knuckles and most other parts of the hand that wields it. These specific sabers are from the American civil-war era, the era that was pretty much the end of their usage on the actual battlefield though they are still used ceremonially in militaries the world-a-round. Oh wait, their aren't many militaries left in the world, don't believe me, go look at the map.

We sent about fifty thousand cavalry troops after the enemy's cavalry, which is far more than they have, and about another fifty thouand toward their flanks too deal with the enemy archers who were still in action firing their arrows, desperately hoping too reduce the numbers of our horse-force. Little do they know that their efforts are invain. Not only will our horse men be in so close that they won't have time too shoot their arrows but our cavalry, just like all our other troops are wearing state of the art, twenty-first century kevlar body vests which their arrows will just stick too as well as bounce off of.

I hear the thundering of the enemies horse hooves pounding off of the hard Earth. The screams of terror as my Byzantine brothers break and run but where do they think they're going too run to? No mere man can outrun a horse let alone a army of them, but I know there's no other choice. I drop my bow and turn to flee. I don't get far before I hear one of the enemy coming upon me from behind. I unsheath my sword as I turn around to face death, but just maybe if I can cut the horse in the legs or stick it in the side just maybe I can bring it to the ground and attack it's rider face to face. It doesn't go down like that. I find myself looking down the hole of a cylinder like hand held object. I hear the sonic boom after I find myself falling to the ground.

Our cavalry as well as all other Epitaph troops, as a back-up weapon are carrying The Gasser Montenegro revolver eighteen seventy-five. This is a Austrian made, ten point seven, five shot, single-action revolver. It's overall length is two hundred sixty-four milimeters and weighs thirty-three ounces. It has a fixed notch sight with a beautiful walnut grip which feels just right in the palm of my hand.

Now that their cavalry is gone and their archers decimated it's time for our own bowmen too step forward and annihilate the enemy infantry who, just like true stubborn Romans are still trying too fight. Our own bowmen, in two lines of one hundred troops each are methadically marching forward. They are using repeating, rapid fire crossbows that were invented in China around two hundred A.D. Now I know these are older weapons but their design is so simple and far advanced that they will be practical for years to come. You just hold the bow close to your body, around the stomach area and drop in the twelve inch iron tipped bolts or arrows into the magazine slot on top. After dropping in the arrows, ten at a time, you manually push the lever forward which moves the magazine with it causing the string to fall into the slotted notch and be drawn back as you bring back the magazine. You push the peg like button which causes the arrow to fly downfield, about eighty yards or so, and if your fast enough you can shoot one arrow per second. When the first line is done they drop down to one knee and reload as the second line shoots. These arrows are more than strong enough to go through the chainmail that the Romans are wearing as they are painfully finding out. As they drop like flies that get just a little too close to a insect light, I with a gleam in my eye decide that the time has come for the final push forward by dispatching my own infantry. The Roman infantry, thanks to their scutums have put up a admirable defense against my bowmen, but they are now shifting out, half to one side, the other half to the other side as so that they can now attack the Roman want-to-be's from their vulnerable flanks as my own infantry charges forward with head-strong determination. The Romans seeing this, know that they can't defend all three sides, and that they will probably soon be completely encircled have decided too fight and hope for the best. They have yet too realize that most of my cavalry is returning and is fixing too hit them from behind so yes, they are completely encircled.

I sit upon my stallion listening too the sweet sounds of Bach and Mozart, I mean the horrific screams of those Byzantine Bastards as they get cut down to shredded meat by my own troops, but to my ears that is the sweet sound of beautiful music. Completely enclosed they have nowhere to run. They're getting pierced by arrows on the flanks. Cut down by sabre baring horsemen from behind, and sliced and diced from sword wielding infantry from the front. Ah their loud, bellowing yells do bring pleasure to me. Now that we've reclaimed the west it's time too push east. Straight into the heart of The Eastern Roman Empire.

Unfortunately my next assignment put me at sea. I don't really care to be on water that much. Guess I'm just not too fond of it. I prefer too be a land mammal only. I like the comforting feel of hard ground beneath my feet. But it's all good. I have with me the best naval commander of all time. Infact she is the supreme naval commander of all Epitaph Naval Forces. Artemesia. This five foot four light, bronzed skin beauty with bouncy, black hair that flows to her mid-back was for a spell Queen of Caria. A area that was at one time a protectorate of the Persian Empire. This made her a reluctant adviser to Xerxes, The Persian ruler. Yeah, he was a little odd, or out of touch with reality. Before every meal he ate he would have a servant whisper into his ear, "Sir, don't forget the Athenians." A few years later, when a storm destroyed the bridge he had built across the Hellespont he ordered that the sea recieve five hundred lashes with the whip. Yeah! You should've seen the look on the faces of the two who had too carry that order out. They already thought the king was a few fries shy of a happy meal, now they knew he was completely off his rocker. And when Artemesia in the middle of battle brilliantly made a daring escape by ramming and sinking both enemy and allie ships alike Xerxes never even realized it. He applauded her bravery and scolded the rest of his naval commanders by besmirching them with the words "My men are becoming women, and my women are becoming men!" Artemesia's life, in her opinion eventually became dull and uneventful. After Xerxes failed attempt at conquering mainland Greece in four-eighty B.C. he didn't have a need for many naval commanders. He spent the remainder of his years putting down internal revolts. This left Artemesia with too much time on her hands and not enough of a itinerary too fill her days. She tried filling the void in her life by taking lovers and consorts but even this failed to bring her fulfillment. However when she was at her lowest point, convinced that life was no-longer worth living and that the time too say goodbye to this world has come is when he came to her. No, not me. Epitaph decided to field this one himself, can't blame him. On a beauty scale of one to ten she is at least a twelve, if not a fourteen. He artfully persuaded her to join the cause and made it appear that she, like so many others just simply vanished from the pages of history. Of course she didn't disappear. She's standing here with me right now in the Sea Of Marmara on board a sixteenth century galleon.

The year is six seventy-seven A.D. and for the last five years The Byzantines have been constantly harassed on both land and sea by Arabics who have been united under the new flag of the budding religion of Islam. The push westward from their homeland on the Arabian peninsula had brought them in direct conflict with The Eastern Romans and this is the year they decided too pick up the pace. They were still making small land raids against Byzantine held territory as well as attacking Byzantine merchant ships but now they came to the conclusion that a empire can't fight if that empire is starving. This prompted them to sternly put up a harsh, inflexible, unrelenting blockade on the south side of the Bosporus strait, completely isolating Constantinople from all incoming ships of anykind. It didn't take The Eastern Romans long too start feeling the pressure that was being applied by the Arabic blockade. Almost everything that went through-out The Eastern Roman Empire at one-time or another traveled threw Constantinople. This was having crippling effects on the empire as a whole but the impact is being felt ten-fold in Constantinople itself. The local economy came to a abrupt and sudden halt. Traders and salesmen of all kinds suddenly found themselves out of business. Most with nothing to fall back on. Many shops and vendors sat idle or completely shut-down. However there was very little looting or pillaging. The emperor, Constantine The Fourth, had enough sense too stockpile food and money so the people of the city did recieve daily rations. The blockade lasted a good two and -a-half to three months. Thats how long it took the emperor too fully mobilize his fleets that were in the Black Sea at the beginning of the Arabic blockade. Having centralized all his ships to the south side of the Black Sea it is now time to sail threw the Bosporus and punch through the Arabic's maritime barricade, relieving the capital city of Constantinople. Once outside the Bosporus Strait the Byzantine ships immediately navigated into a semi-circler pattern which in the seventh century is standard formation. Also immediate once exiting The Bosporus was the visibility of the Arabic forces. The Romans push-on in their warships, hell bent on destroying their foe. The Roman warships or Dromon comes in a few different versions but the ones they're using here are all about the same. Fifty meters long and five meters wide with two tiers. The bottom deck is for the oarsmen only. Fifty of them and you don't want too be one of them. The stale, stenchy air your forced to breath in. The sweaty, stinky individual your sitting beside. And yourself. The sweat and grime that is emanating from your own foul smelling body. The top tier isn't much better even though you at least do have fresh air too breath. You'll be rowing up here as well even though there are sails. Unless your one of the marines stationed aboard the ship you'll be rowing until the time of battle when you'll then turn into a maritime warrior. You'll probably be on the deck level though some of you will be on the tower that is located almost dead center of the ship. The sails are lateen sails but unless your familiar with boats it's probably easier too think of them as side-ways triangles. Atop the towers will be many men throwing rocks, spears, metal, anything they can grab. Many will also be shooting bows and arrows and if available this is where the catapults will be put. Most of the ships will also have a siphon up front so that they can dispense their new terrifying weapon, greek fire. Now I know what your thinking, Caesarian, just not too long ago you said they hadn't yet invented greek fire. Not the grenade version, just the liquid fire version, it's still over a hundred years till one of these Romans grows a brain and realizes it can also be used on land but even this version they're using now is in it's infancy. Greek fire is the one thing the Arabs don't have, other than that the two fleets are almost identical. The Muslim ships look very similar too their Roman counterparts except they're a wee-bit wider and therefore heavier which also equals slower. So out of the Bosporus they come, steaming toward their adversaries. Both navies firing their catapults, hurling heavy projectiles at one another. The first tier oarsmen are frantically heaving and rowing making the stale air even more unbearable with their hot, heavy breathing. The sweat pouring off of their brows like cascading water over a waterfall. But in a way the battle depends on these men more than those doing the actual fighting. These are the ones who are the difference makers. They have too be physically fit cause if they give out, even with the lateen sails if it ain't a good, windy day the ship will be stranded motionless. The two navies are getting closer to one another while still using the catapults but now there also in range for arrows too be effective. It won't be long at all till the hand thrown projectiles can come into play but the Arabs are still moving closer toward the Romans. They don't know they're falling into a trap because they're not familiar with greek fire. They are still use too the old ways of naval battle. Which is to get in close to your enemy and either ram him or board him and hopefully take the ship rather than sink it but greek fire can be used from a distance of only a few dozen feet away and once your in that close it's far too late to escape.

I stand here behind my mounted siphon at the bow of the ship with my commander beside me waiting for him too give the order. These towel head Muslims invaders are lined up in a straight line thinking they can just punch right threw our cresent shape formation. Ha, ha do we have a surprise for them, if only they knew. They're getting closer now. Spears and arrows flying all around me. From time to time I have too duck to avoid being pierced by one of these airborne projectiles but then I heard my commanders order. "Fire!" "Fire, isn't that funny?" So fire I do, quite literally. I gleefully watch with much fascination as the firey, liquid stream protrudes from the bronze tube at almost two thousand degrees fahrenheit, incendiarying everything in it's wake. I pivot the bronze tube both up and down as well as back and forth in a sweeping motion just so I can terrorize my enemies even more. I love my job, I love exterminating enemies of Eastern Rome. Not only are the enemy ships engulfed in flames swimming upon the sea like giant, floating ashtrays but as a extra bonus I can actually see some of those Muslims on fire running around as if they are human torches. Hey, what do you know, those turban tops they wear are good for something, they make excellent wicks. Just look at that Arabic burn. How do you like your infidel? Burnt or extra crispy? And the cloth robes they wear, they make great kindling, heck it causes those Muslims to go up like Roman candles. However as gratifying as it is too see our enemies in pain the smell on the other hand is nasty. The combined foul, rancid, putrid scent of burning hair and flesh is not pleasing in any way. Not only are your nostrils overcome with a sulfuric, rotten egg smell that is just so nauseating that you almost wanna puke but that invading, grotesque smell also has a way of somehow assaulting your taste buds, leaving a taste you never want too know and a taste you just can't never seem to get rid of. Oh, hey, look, they have back-up units. Alright, more Muslims too burn.

I'm standing on the deck of Artemesia's flagship with the Carian queen at my side. We are coming up from behind of whats left of the Muslim navy, this way both them and the Romans are directly in front of us, trapped at the mouth of the strait and even if the Romans do try to escape by going up the Bosporus well, then, hey, whatever. I'm sure we'll be happy to pursue, though they don't have a chance. Sixteenth century galleons are far faster than anything them Byzantine bastards have seen outside of maybe a shooting star streaking across the heavens. After all they are built for speed. Starting with the hull which is wider at the waterline but slopes and tapers inward, getting slimmer as it rises to the top. This puts the weight toward the center of the ship, unlike those slow, snail like cadillacs the enemy has. The flat narrow stern also helps by giving us far more maneuverability than our cumbersome adversaries. Also unlike our foes we can jet along at about eight knots, thanks too the vastly improved sail rigging. Our only drawback is that we run strickley on nothing but wind power. No sweaty oarsmen over here. We are also heavily armed. Thirty cannons on each side of the ship and one mounted aft. The cannons we have are more than adequate for this mission of unmercy. The medium sized demi-cannon. They are eleven feet long, weighing fifty-six hundred pounds apiece. They have a caliber of six to six and a-half inches with a range of almost sixteen-hundred feet. As we approach closer we turn to our broadside, our ships lining up one behind another, getting ready too unleash our fury.

Whats with this Arabic back-up support? It looks like they're turning to flee already. Darn! There goes my fun. I wanted too toast more towel heads. I must say though, those are some funny looking ships. I've never seen anything like them, but hey, who knows what goes through the minds of those Muslims.

With our eighty galleons facing broadside toward both of the other navies we indiscriminately let loose with our massive amount of cannon fire, sinking both Roman and Muslim alike. After all I could care less how many of them die by sinking to a watery grave. Hopefully they all will. I have no love for Romans or Arabics. Yeah, I despise the Romans with great hatred but my people have had run-ins with these Arabs since before Menes brought us together.

Oh shit! Those aren't Muslims. It must be that dreaded devil's horde, The Army Of Darkness or something like that. Up till now I thought they were just a legend. They're raising their colors now. A bright red flag with a black outline of the mighty Epitaph looking at his mirror image with a glass held high, toasting himself. Black on red, are those not the colors of Satan? Oh well, I gotta get out of here. Do I just jump over, right into the sea and hope for the best or do I take the time too grab one of those canoe like life boats? Hell with it. I'm jumping.

Ha, ha! Look at all those sinking ships. I love listening too the enemy scream, knowing that their cries are in vain. Those that don't drown on their own won't be screaming much longer. I've posted sharpshooters on the fighting platforms that are half-way up the mast poles, and thats merciful if they don't get hit by one of the volleys of cannon fire that we keep spewing out of the demi-cannons. Some of the Romans have somehow managed to get little canoe like boats into the water and are trying desperately to reach land. Like they're actually gonna make it. He, he thats what the sloops are here for. To stop that from happening. Sloops can go into very shallow waters and even if those Romans do make land, thats okay. We've got troops there waiting for them so it's not like they have a chance. As for those few Roman Dromons that did try to flee we also had with us some undersea beasts. Yeah, o.k., submarines.

All thats left now is floating, wooden debris on the waters surface of what used too be Roman and Muslim warships. There's also a few floating cadavers. Some face up and some face down. A few of them are even starting too bloat out from all the water that particular victim swallowed. Yeah, there's even still patches of greek fire sporadically burning here and there as though they are little oil lamps set adrift too light the way to hell for all the damned souls that have fallen here today. I turn toward Artemesia, handing her a chalice of ruby red wine with my left hand and raising my own cup with my right, "Not bad for a days work. "

We let loose our land troops so that they can capture Anatolia, thats Turkey too you, and continue south through the holy land. Gobbling up North Africa as well as anything else that may have belonged too Eastern Rome. All thats left now is Constantinople and all Byzantine lands north of the city.

Starting in the year one thousand Basil The Second turned his attention west in a all out invasion of Bulgaria. Slowly but surely, step by step the Byzantine menace pushed on. They continued to take towns and territory almost at will. Finally in one thousand five, even though the Bulgarians were by now on the defensive the Byzantine war machine had idled down to a snails pace. Gains were minimal at best for the next eight years. However in ten-fourteen the Eastern Roman emperor summoned up a hugh army of a hundred thousand men, almost three times the size of a normal military in those days. He then moved through the Bulgarian countryside along the banks of the Struma river. From here he entered into the Strmitsa valley and onward to the Belasitsa and Ozgrazhden mountains. The mountain range sits on the corner of what will be Greece, Macedonia, and Bulgaria but as of now this is all disputed land between The Bulgarian Empire and yep, you guessed it, them Byzantine Bastards, The Eastern Romans. The mountains themselves are about sixty kilometers long and their highest point, Radomir, is two thousand twenty-nine meters. The borders of the above mentioned countries meet at Tunba Peek which has a elevation of six thousand, one hundred and sixty-eight feet. It has a nice, rounded dome at the top as though it could almost be a natural cathedral for all of the people of the Balkans too take a pilgrimage to.

The Romans don't get too far into the mountains when they stumble upon the Bulgarians who have been waiting with much anticipation. They know it's now or never, that the Romans have too be stopped here. The Byzantines have found themselves looking at a makeshift fort of somekind. The Bulgarians have walled themselves in with a sturdy, wooden palisade, completely blocking the north and south narrow paths through the mountains. They are also using the steep, mountainous, bluffs too protect their east and west flanks. Their's also both guard and lookout towers equally spaced around the inside of the perimeter that gives the Bulgarians a bit of a visibility advantage which they need since they are vastly outnumbered.

Basil decided too test the strength of the palisade with a all-out charge but before the Byzantines even reached the walls they were greeted by falling into a deep, wide, man made ditch that was cleverly concealed with brush and twigs by the Bulgarians. With the air being pierced by the sounds of both horses whining and neighing, as well as that of full grown men yelling and screaming as they plummet down into the false gulley those Bulgarians in the towers, that were close enough to the chaos let loose with one wave after another of arrows that showered down onto both man and beast as he tries too arise. Very few escaped, forcing the Byzantines to lay siege to the Bulgarian stronghold.

The first few days of the siege were, for the most part pretty dull and uneventful. The Byzantines would charge up toward the Bulgarian barricade in a feinted attack while trying desperately too stay out of range of the Bulgarian arrows. In actuality they were trying too figure out just how wide that Bulgarian ditch really is. By the end of the first week however the terror became real for the Bulgarians. The Byzantines had managed too haphazardly slap together a few catapults and are currently hurling giant stones at the Bulgarian stronghold. This continued for the next few weeks until the reinforcements that Basil had sent for finally arrived out of Thessalonika. During the siege the Romans had built both ladders and battering rams too break through the Bulgarian defenses. They will use the ladders to cross the ditch and once all the men and battering rams are across they will pick-up the ladders then use them too scale the palisade walls. While this is happening the recently arrived reinforcements will use one of the dangerous mountain passes to circle behind the Bulgarians and hit them from behind, overwhelming them in a pincer like movement. The Byzantines are all gathered up, ready too put their plan into action when we sprang forth from our places of concealment in the rough, ridgedy mountain tops. We simultaneously let loose with both snipers who are once again using the gewehr ninty-eight and a company of the Epitaph Terror Squad who are using the knee mortar. These troops have been strategically placed in mountains on both sides of the path-like roadway that the Byzantines occupy.

The Byzantines probably believe that the sky is falling in on them. I'll bet they never imagined it would be anything like this, what too them must seem like a nightmarish hell that is raining down upon them. The explosions going off all around them. Their friends and comrades laying in both pieces and pools of blood. And the holes. The holes that simultaneously develop when what too them is a form of deviltry that hits the Earth. They must be wondering, who's work is this? I would guess that they know by now that it can't be the Bulgarians. Oh shit, they're starting too beat feet out of here, I gotta go!

For the next three and-a-half weeks we played a fun little game of cat and mouse with the Eastern Romans. Once chaos and hell erupted all about them they did all they could too try and make it back to Constantinople, but until they got out of the mountains progress on their part was very slow. We shadowed or followed them from a safe distance and continued too harass them by sniping them out when they least expected it. They were all scared to death not knowing if it would be them that would drop down dead next by the unseen enemy. I find it comical knowing that by the end of the first week they were blaming one-another for bringing this demonic plague of death down upon them. Many a-nights they would break out into downright fist fights by the night-time campfire. Some of them would actually end up in the fire, smelting the chainmail to their flesh only to leave permanent little circles on the parts of their skin where they had inadvertently branded themselves. It was like watching a cross between WWE Wrestling and Ultimate Fighting Championship until swords and other weapons would come into play. But by then Basil and his elite guards would quickly put a stop too all of this. Just in the first week alone my snipers must have picked off almost ten-thousand of those raunchy, want-to-be Roman scumbags as they tried to make their way back home, where they thought they would be safe.

Until they reached Constantinople we continued too routinely bag our limit of Romans. They were dropping like flies through the scopes of my sharpshooters. However, unfortunately, they eventually made it inside the city walls. They must think that those walls will actually stop us from getting in. Stupid Romans.

They have good reason too feel secure behind those walls of their's. After all, the city itself had never been sacked by a foreign military of anykind. We approached the city from the west and the first sight you behold is the Theodosian Wall. The wall goes the whole way around the city perimeter and there's a immense size moat that lays before it. Even when you do get across the moat you still have to find a way too scale the wall that now stands before you. Okay, your now over that obstacle. Now you better run as fast as you can cause it's a good distance till you reach the next wall, which is yet even taller. If you actually make it over this one, run Forest run. Run like the wind, because in front of you is the great, behemoth wall of them all. It's over thirty feet tall and sixteen and a-half feet thick. It also has ninty-six towers and each tower is not only well manned but over sixty feet tall. Only after breaching all of these barriers will you then be able to penetrate your way into the city. But good luck with all of this. You have too achieve these feats while being showered with Roman arrows. They may even be, and I hope not, throwing the Greek Fire grenades at you. From within the city they will be hurling giant size boulders at you from both catapults and trebuchets. I think a snowball has a better chance of making it through hell then you do through this medieval obstacle course.

The beachfront piece of real-estate that Constantinople sits on was originally founded by Greek colonists in the seventh century B.C. They named it Byzantium after their leader Byzas. Though others had been there before the Greeks, they had long ago abandoned the place and it had changed hands more than once before falling under Roman tyranny.

The city has been attacked many times and therefore these Romans know how too handle it. They're always well stocked with both food and water. Even though on our way here we blew-up the aqueducts that flow into the city that just effectively stops the flow of more water into the city but they can still hold-out for who knows how long. The water, upon entering Constantinople use to flow into a underground system of cisterns where it will stay until someone at ground level pumps it out.

When Basil returned and advised the people too prepare most of them thought "Great, another siege. How long will this one last?" They knew this ment everything will come to a screeching halt, and that food will once again be rationed. What they didn't know is that this is going too be a siege unlike anything they ever experienced before.

Unfortunately this will be the last Roman stronghold I get to seize for awhile, so of course I'm going too pull out all of the stops and make this well worth it. Sure! I'll start off routinely but I'll escalate too something these Romans have never seen or experienced before. Oh the fun and joy of spreading death and destruction, how great it can be. I've once again brought up the twenty-four pound, smoothbore cannons since they're more then adequate for the job. After all, they can hurl their projectiles over twice the distance of any trebuchet. "Fire!"

Wow! I've seen foreign armies try too attack our city before but nothing like this. They use weapons I've never seen or even heard of in all my days. Weapons that can be conjured up only by the devil himself. When I was a child my parents would tell my siblings and me of tales about a mythical phantom army. A army that would blaze a wanton path of destruction and pulverize everything in it's wake, leaving nothing behind but rubble and ruin. Could this really be that said army. That unnamed army of death and destruction that everyone fears. It's only taken them about a week too smash holes in the first wall of defense, something no other foe has done before. Holes more than big enough for a man to get through. Usually the city walls are well garrisoned with our own troops but they can't stand up too these kinds of weapons. They had to pull back to within the city gates with us civilians, and just like the rest of us the only thing they can do is wait and hope for the best. Hope that the remaining last two walls can somehow stop them.

Progress has been made but much slower than I had anticipated. Unfortunately these Romans know how too build. They made these walls out of limestone and mortar mixed with brick. That's okay. Their first line of defense has fallen and the second one isn't far from it, however I dare not to send my troops forward. I'm not dumb enough too fall into that trap. Once within range they'll surely let loose with those catapults and trebuchets of theirs. Once that second wall fall's I'll step up the terror once again putting too good use the knee mortar.

We thought things were bad enough when all we could do was standback helplessly and watch our fortifications crumble to dust but now these evil manifestations have somehow called upon the sky to rain down fire upon us. I don't know what kind of magic they use but surely it is not pure. Luckily the sky screams before this cataclysmic chaos falls on us. Barely giving us enough time to run for cover, but this doesn't mean that you'll be safe from instant annihilation. Many buildings burst out in fierce explosions, throwing debris everywhere before collapsing down upon themselves, left only to lay in a rubbish pile of rocks and bricks. Great clouds of chronic smoke rise up to strangle the clean air and linger like a thick fog through-out the city, leaving you to gasp and choke for the fresh breath of life. Ear splitting blasts echo and repeat all around me as all I know is layed to waste. Friends and strangers both lie on the rubble soiled ground either already dead or begging in agony for death to take them. Why and how is it that I've been spared through...

I've been shelling their city for almost a week now while simultaneously knocking down their walls with my trusty cannons. The first two lines of defense have fallen and there is actually holes in the last of their great walls for my men too get threw. It's now time for the final stage.

Oh my lord, I thought I have seen it all, until now. I can't believe what my eyes behold. That satanic army that has attacked our great city and destroyed all that I've ever called home has sent giant birds that at this very moment are flying by overhead while dropping down on us demon soldiers. Thats correct! Real soldiers are falling from the sky. And not just a few, thousands of them! I would run and hide, but where? We can't stop this, there's not enough of us left. They'll overrun the city in no time. And they're falling from the sky! Who ever heard of such a thing. Oh no! I can see one of them landing now. I better get out of here!

Even though all of their walls have come tumbling down I, as of yet dare not to send my forces forward. I know there can't be many more Romans left but those few that are may put their trebuchets too use by taking out some of my men. No sense in losing good Epitaph Troops. Thats why I sent in my paratroopers, once they overrun the city me and the ground forces can move in.

I called upon the German World War Two Messerschmitt Me three twenty-three heavy transport plane. Being that it was the largest land-based transport plane of the war it is a slow, cumbersome, bulky aircraft that if pitted against post World War Two air vehicles it would suffer many casulties. With a maximum speed of just over one hundred and seventy miles per hour it definitely won't set no records getting from point A to point B. It weighs between sixty and sixty-five thousand pounds and has a average range of five hundred miles. With it's wingspan of one hundred and eighty-one feet it's more like a airbus than a airplane and in a effort too shave off some weight most of the wings are made of plywood and fabric. I don't think they succeeded though since it has six mounted engines. Three that rotate clockwise and three that rotate the other way. The cargo hold itself is thirty-six feet long and ten feet wide and can hold somewhere in the area of one hundred and thirty troops.

Yes. The Epitaph paratroopers who are dropping from these airbeasts are equipped with modern kevlar suits, boots, and even gloves. They also carry with them minor items such as The Epitaph Battle Dagger, water canteen, compass, U.S. style World War Two Pineapple grenades, etc. The first thing that will stand out too you if your a Roman scumbag trapped in Constantinople is the World War One gas masks strapped across the face of the paratrooper before you. These gas masks are just like the ones used in the Metaurus campaign except here they serve no purpose what-so-ever other than too trick the Romans into believing that they face unhuman adversaries. Now the firearm of choice is the FG-Forty-Two Battle Rifle. Yes, once again I turned to World War Two Germany. What can I say, they have cool weapons. The FG-Forty-Two, with the flip of a switch is either semi or full auto. It's gas operated and has a twenty round magazine that sticks out on the left side of the rifle. It's average weight is ten pounds and it's thirty-eight inches long. It fires a variant of a seven point ninty-two milimeter shell and has a rate of fire of seven to nine hundred rounds per minute and a effective range of five hundred meters.

The demon soldiers known as Beelzebub's Boys descended down into the great city as the fallen angels they are. They tore through the metropolis as though they were a category five hurricane, laying waste too all that stood before them. It mattered not if it was human or not, it didn't even matter if it had ever lived or not. All too these beings was fair in war and war. If you were too have walked threw the city that day after they were done with their barbaric fun you would have thought a dam had broke. A dam that held back a river of blood for you would've found yourself standing in thick blood noless than ankle deep. The bodies of both men and animals lay everywhere, not one of them in it's entirety. All of them were missing something. Hands, head, feet, fingers, something. And the wretched smell of fresh guts and sinew would almost make you choke and gasp. I only hope and pray for you that Beelzebubs Boy's never come to your town.

Now that all of Rome has finally fallen there's only one more thing I wish too do. One more thing I need too do!

Six seventy-seven A.D. All of North Africa and The Holy Land has been wrested from the grip of Roman tyranny. The Islamic Muslims have been beaten back to their homeland and the peoples of the land are emphatically rejoicing. Then it dawned on them "Who are our rulers, who was strong enough too defeat the Romans and the Arabics at the same time?" Epitaph heralders soon answered those questions when they delivered the news that they now belong to the Epitaph Empire and that they are now subjects of the Epitaph himself. You should have seen the fear on their faces, but they knew they were helpless. Too revolt would be certain and swift death.

The people of Egypt also recieved a message from Epitaph. A message that said not only are they now free of Rome but as a reward their new leader will be arriving soon. That he is a pure blooded pharaoh and that they will be allowed too return to their old ways. Thats right. I'm coming home!

Alexanderia: Six Seventy-Seven A.D.

My people lined the streets. Eagerly chanting and cheering, waving signs that read "Welcome Back Pharaoh." Of course they were all wondering "A Pharaoh?" "Of pure blood?" Who is he? What is he going to look like?

I started the celebratory festivities by having beautiful Egyptian maidens toss a abundant amount of lotuses into the air. The Egyptian lotus is as white as pure snow. There is a blue version but I choose to go with white too represent the rebirth of the new Egypt. The Egypt that is controlled by me and ruled by Epitaph. Next to come is the male servants. They toss bread and biscuits into the crowds out of huge, weaved baskets that they proudly carry. Don't worry, no-one is going too get thirsty. I've got bronze Egyptian babes handing out ice cold beer and other refreshments to the gleeful masses. After all, beer has been the drink of choice for us Egyptians for thousands of years now. It's about time the rest of you all catch on too the good stuff. Now is when the real part of the procession begins. It all starts with the first of four standards, thats little flags too all you lmao's out there. Obviously you have no military experience at all. They are all a dull, dark red in color. The first one has two words in white letters in the center, one directly above the other. Shay and Shait. Those are two different versions of the same Ancient Egyptian deity. Shay the male, Shait the female. They stand for fate and destiny and this is the destiny of Egypt as well as the Egyptians, too be mine as they should have all those centuries ago. Underneath the spelled out words in white outline is the picture of both a snake and a pig. Yes, male and female. The next standard in line has a white outline of a Sema running straight down the center. The Sema represents the unification of Egypt that too you all was a little over five thousand years ago. It could look like a windpipe with your lungs nailed to it but it's really a solid stick with the lotus of Upper Egypt and the Papyrus of Lower Egypt tied to it. Now instead of a white outline the third standard is done in black and it's the Sign Of Totality which is a snake, in a circle swallowing it's own tail. This stands for continuity and immortality. Unity and infinity which has no beginning and no end. This is what Epitaph is, Endless! The last of the four standards is also outlined in black, The Shen Symbol. The Shen, just like the Symbol Of Totality is a circle, but the Shen is a endless circle of rope twined around itself. It also represents all, eternity, everything, infinity. Now is the procession of Egypt's Gods. First in the divine line-up is the holy and sacred cow, Heset. To put on exhibit Heset herself I had a real live New Jersey Dairy Cow. She was fawn in color and had patches of both white and dark brown. She weighed about one thousand pounds and had black hooves on her feet. Since Heset is the goddess of plenty I had a tray strapped to her head. Believe me, it was all kinds of fun trying too get her to cooperate for that. Anyhow, on the tray was all kinds of food and treats, bread, grapes, crackers, fish, I also had handed out to the crowds, fresh from the udder milk, but too get anyone to actually drink it I had too market it as "Beer Of Heset." Next up, on a cart being towed by camels, just like most of the remaining deities is a three and-a-half foot wooden statue of the god, Thoth. Thoth is shown too have the body of a man with the head of a Ibis. Now I know that unless you live in a tropical region your probably wondering what is a Ibis. It's a large bird that hangs out near bodies of water and has long legs with a very long, slender, curved bill. Thoth is the god of knowledge and wisdom as well as writing and language. He is often shown holding a scribe's palette and stylus. Upon your death he is the one who questions you about your life's deeds before your heart is weighed against the Feather Of Maat. Thoth is here too demonstrate to my people that as long as they are loyal servants to Epitaph and myself that they shall be privy to knowledge beyond their wildest dreams. Knowledge that shall not predate the twentieth century which too them will seem like magic. The number three deity is Maat. She is the goddess of truth, justice, righteousness and her name means "Straight." She'll give you no bullpuckey so unless you want too know the unsugared truth don't ask her no questions. She's pictured as a tall woman with a ostrich-feather in her hair, you know the feather that someday your heart will be weighed against. She's here too show that to follow Epitaph is to follow the truth. To follow the way. The righteous way. Number four is Horus, the falcon headed deity. He is the patron and protector of the living ruler, The Pharaoh. Oh, hey, wait, that would be me. Legend says that in battle he lost his right eye which since then has gone on too become very symbolic, known as The Eye Of Horus. It represents strength, vigor, and self-sacrifice which is everything I am to Egypt and my people. Horus is here to signify my birth-right too rule the land of Egypt. Moving on to number five and please try to refrain from laughter. Next up in my procession is Maqet, that's correct, a ladder. Now I know you would think it silly too see amongst all these wooden deities a twenty foot aluminum ladder come strolling on by but yes it's here none-the-less. In Ancient Egyptian religion Maqet, or the ladder was used to climb up to Nut, the sky goddess and since the sky goes on forever this ladder represents the endless reach of Epitaph. Next up is Geb, Egyptian God Of The Earth. He took the form of a bearded man and was often shown reclining. He could also be personified as Fertile Earth or Barren Desert. He is also the husband of Nut and he is here too show that Epitaph rules the Earth. Now the next divine being from the Egyptian pantheon was the most important god in Ancient Egypt for he is the sun god, the giver of life, Ra. He is the creator of all the other gods and goddess and because he too was a falcon headed deity him and Horus were often mistaken for one another. Here's how you tell them apart. Ra always has a sun disk above his head and Horus will never have one. He is why the west side of The Nile is known as the Land Of The Dead. It was believed he was born each morning in the east and at night dies in the west as he travels through the underworld. It's believed Ra's powers are so great he can literally do anything, no matter what it may be. Which is exactly why he is here, too represent Epitaphs limitless power. Now here is a divinity that many of your twenty-first century nations should call upon, Sopdu. He too is a bird god except he is usually depicted as a full crouching falcon but he can be pictured as a human warrior with long hair and falcon feathers sticking from that fringey frizz of his. He also had with him a battle axe and sword. Yes, he is a god of war but a defensive warrior for he is the divine border patrol agent of Ancient Egypt. Like I said, something a lot of your twenty-first century nations need. He is here too represent the new found protection my people shall enjoy through Epitaph and myself. Now is the blue bodied, bearded man who carries a symbol of long life in one hand and wears another palm frond in his hair. He is the motionless, primordial waters that begot Ra, so therefore he is the reason that life exists. He is here too show that Epitaph is the beginning. It is unfortunate that this next deity is even here, but he has to be. Osiris that is, Lord Of The Dead. He got bounded to these duties when he himself was killed by Seth. Though he is still a animate being he is no longer considered a living god and therefore must now dwell in the underworld. He is often portrayed as a green, mummified pharaoh and is praised by the souls of those who pass the test of the weight of the feather. He is here too protect dead Epitaph troops, what few there are. Since I just mentioned Seth a few sentences ago I'll take the time and space to address him here and now. He is the god of violence and chaos. outright hostility and beyond evil. He purposefully creates calamities for mortals and gods alike just for his amusement and something to do. He is shown with the body of a man but his head is not of this world. His face has a long, curved snout, almost like a bird's beak, and square-tipped ears that stand straight-up. He also has a very long, forked tail. He is here too demonstrate the wrath that will befall you if you wrong Epitaph in any way. Next is a war goddess and with her she brings vast amounts of widespread vengence and destruction. There's just something about women warriors that lights my fire. I don't know what it is but they make my loins leap with joy. However not this goddess. She has a body that is all woman but she sports the head of a lioness. Sekhmet is her name and she is here too represent the destruction that will befall you if you cross Epitaph. Next is yet another falcon headed deity. Not only does this one have a sun disk above his head but there's two plumes that extend from it so as not too be confused with the other sun disked, falcon headed deity, Ra. Monthu is also a god of war. He is very destructive and will lay waste to all before him. You will abruptly know if you offend or enrage him for his falcon head will morph into the head of a bull. To us Egyptians he represents strength, virility, and victory. He is shown to hold many different kinds of weapons in his hands. He is here too show that through Epitaph I have the right to make war against whoever I choose. Now comes the one that all Egyptians fear, no matter what! He is the bringer of darkness, death, and all that is evil. He was often referred to as "The Serpent From The Nile." Now almost all Egyptian gods, in one way or another are worshipped, even Seth, but not Apep. If anything, he was anti-worshipped. I guess in a attempt to banish him forever. In the old days my people would make wax or mud models of Apep and then spit on them, defecate on them, burn them, and mutilate them, anything to wish ill against Apep. So when the people seen that he is on display a silent hush fell over the crowd. Their eyes bugged out as their jaws hit the ground. Who could be so powerful as to cage the mighty Apep? The snake that is on display that they think is Apep is enclosed in a clear, thick plastic aquarium that is twice his length. This is a snake that no Egyptian has seen before, so now you know why they are flabbergasted as well as convinced they're looking at Apep. I have with me a twenty-eight foot, South American anaconda that weighs in excess of five hundred pounds and is just a little under four feet around. Yeh, he gives me the heebie-jeebies as well. Trust me, I don't go near him. He is here too show that Epitaph can be The Great Destroyer of everything. Now even as Apep passes from view the crowds are still silent for they now see who has the power to cage Apep. Now when I extended the invitation I never expected it to be honored but here he is before my people, Epitaph! No, not a statue of him, but The Epitaph himself. Being that he stands at about six foot, seven he towers over the wooden Egyptian deities as he passes by with his robes following behind him on the ground. His hood pulled so far down that you can't possibly see who he is or what he looks like. He wears black gloves to cover his hands as he clutches his sacred book. His button device dangles from his belt-loops along with his dagger, compass, canteen, and phone. I don't know if my people have heard of him and recognize him or if they somehow instinctively know that he is the one, but as one unit they drop to their knees. Their faces down and hands extended before them with their palms on the ground, they pay homage to their New Master.

Even though Epitaph has passed by the people remain on their knees but they do sit-up to lay their eyes upon their new Pharaoh. It is I, with a little gap between us that follows directly behind Epitaph. I am in my war chariot being pulled by a bright, white stallion. The dull red standard flying high above my chariot baring my name in big, bright, white letters. As my chariot passes the crowds I confidently stand before my people, dressed in my best. I am wearing the first thing that probably comes to your mind when you hear the word Pharaoh and that would be the Nemes. The black and yellow striped headcloth that covers my whole head and hangs down to my back with two large lappets that hang behind my ears and down over my shoulders. On top of the Nemes is the Pschent, or the Double Crown. It combined the crowns of lower and upper Egypt and represents the Pharaoh's power over all of Egypt. It has two animals on the front. A Egyptian cobra in the ready to strike position and the Egyptian vulture. Together they are referred to as "The Two Ladies." This crown has been around since Egypt was first unified. I only wish mom could be here to see this. She would be so proud of me now! So proud to witness this victory celebration as well as my coronation. My rise to Pharaoh-hood. Next is gold necklaces that brightly shine in the sunlight as they adorn my neck. They almost blind anyone who looks directly upon me. In one of the leather armbands that are wrapped around me I have a few Ostrich feathers stuck under them. Ostrich feathers symbolize truth and justification. In my hands I carry two wooden scepters. The first known as the Sekhem, which represents my authority and the Was, which stands for my power. I also have a leather vest on which I had too cut slots into so that I could strap two items to my chest. The Crook and the Flail. The Crook to you is what you would think of as a cane. A cane with a hooked handle. The Flail is a rod with three strands of beads. It would look kinda like A Cat Of Nine Tails, except this is no weapon. To Egyptians nothing says royalty more than these two symbols. I also have on a yellowish, white cloth kilt. A KILT! Not a skirt, and unless you want to find yourself staked out in the desert you'll continue too humor me and call it a kilt. I had special loops made on my kilt so I can carry the rest of my items. First is the ankh, which is the Egyptian symbol of life. Next is the Khepresh. The War Crown. Like the Nemes it's made of cloth except this one is blue in color. It was worn into battle by many Pharaohs. Now is just my common items. Compass, canteen, dagger, phone. On my feet I have what all my fore-fathers would be wearing. Sandals. After me, on a camel pulled cart are servants tossing gold coins into the crowd. Coins just like those that were given to the Romans during my parade in Rome. Even though these ones have the silhouette of Epitaph on the one side just like the Roman coins the picture of me is different on this coin. On the one given to the Romans I was dressed as a Caesar but on this new coin i'm dressed as a Pharaoh. In a grand, spectacular finish I had fireworks set-off as if it were The Fourth Of July and just as I figured my people were awed and spellbound. But unfortunately all good things must come to a end and i'll eventually have to leave home even though I don't want too. Ever!

Part IV

Clarity

When we arrived at Camp Atterbury we nervously flashed our badges to the guards. I was hoping they would still work, with everything being the way it is I didn't know if they would still be official looking or not. We explained that we were here to collect Billy Williams, which was a weird coincidence since he was being held as a military criminal awaiting transfer and of course Don, being the smooth talker he is, convinced them that we were the ones charged with transporting him. As for the lack of paperwork, according too Don, Billy's crimes involved such sensitive, top secret material, and that since officially this said material doesn't exsist there is too be no followable trail in any way. They had him locked up in one of the buildings that held Krauts and Romans, I mean Germans and Italians back in World War Two. We quickly stuffed Billy into our vehicle and got out of there ASAP.

When asked why he was locked up Billy said it was the strangest thing. Upon returning to base the guards told him that he wasn't on the roster and therefore he didn't belong there. When refusing to leave Billy was arrested for impersonating a soldier. I told him not to worry, that according too Don he's done much worse than that. Billy's reply was "Gee, thanks."

Billy says that he can get us to Lashawn's hometown but outside of that he doesn't know. It's a little rinky-dink place in western Pennsylvania and that when going threw if you blink you might miss it. I bought us a convenience store map just incase we needed it. On the flip side it had in the right hand corner, among other things a small map of the world.

We rented a motel room in Indiana that night and headed out first thing in the morning. It was going to take us the better part of the day to reach P.A. and so we wouldn't be able to start our search for Lashawn till the next day. As we were nearing Pennsylvania I was looking at the map when something caught my attention. That world map that was tucked in the corner had something I had never seen or heard of before. I asked aloud to whoever would answer "Has either of you two ever heard of The Epitaph Empire?" They both answered in unison " The what?" "It's right..." I stopped in mid-sentence. I couldn't believe my eyes. The first time I glanced down this so called Epitaph Empire was only about the size of the Western Roman Empire but now, now it was the size of the entire Roman Empire. It was as if a unknown magician had cast a spell on me from a undisclosed location, or worse yet. A spell upon the world. But how is this possible?

We finally found it. Farrell, Pennsylvania. You talk about a rundown, decrepit looking place, this is it, or at least one of them. It is rinky-dink alright, only about two point three square miles in size. And the crime rate, wow, it is off the charts. It may have a population of only about seven thousand people but it has enough crime too house seven hundred thousand, or at least thats what you would think. Mainly thieves, bandits, and drug dealers, but still there is the occasional murder, at least their not trying too compete with Youngstown, Ohio where there's at least two murders a day, in broad daylight. Still I'll warn all of you caucasians that this is one of the many places that when the sun goes down if your white, DON'T MOVE!

It took us awhile to find the Shell residence and just as I feared he wasn't there. The lady of the house told us that their was however a strange man who came by the other day. Walked straight in her house claiming to be her husband who had just returned from guard duty. She claimed that by the look on his face he seemed genuinely surprised when she told him she has never been married and had never seen him before. We asked her where he went but she said she didn't know, she picked up the phone to call the police but he asked her not too do that as he calmly turned and left.

We scoured the town looking everywhere and asking everyone we saw, even the crackers, which there was lots of, if they knew Lashawn Shell. Of course we turned up nothing and noone seemed to know him. We were about too give up when someone gave us one last location to check. It was in the next town over, Sharon which Farrell is really a suburb of. It was on a street called Bank Place at Joshua's Haven City Mission that we finally found Lashawn. We exited the building strolling across the parking lot all of us thinking, kinda out load, four down only one to go when all of us were suddenly shocked. Casually leaning against our vehicle as if he was Joe Cool was John(Running Dog)Baxter. When asked how he found us all he said was "Dude, I'm a indian." Well, whatever. It saves us the problem of trying to find him.

Running Dog explained that he instantly knew upon entering his reservation that something was not right, something was different. When most of his family didn't recognize him he knew that there was real problems. Real problems that somehow centered around us and where we were at Cades Cove. After much brainstorming we all agreed that our best plan of action was to head back to D.C. and commandeer that truck we had stashed which contained all that knowledge of what was at one time happening at Cades Cove. Luckily Don still has the keys.

We got the truck, which is about as big as a mid-size u-haul. In the five to six days that we were gone noone seemed to pay the truck any mind or attention. I thought for sure it would've been towed but somehow it wasn't even tagged. We hauled ass until we reached the southern part of Virginia where we rented a hotel room. It was actually a pretty spacious room with two beds and a decent sized bathroom off to the side but still this is one of those times that it's kinda awkward being the only female in the group. We started sifting through the many boxes of the different kinds of data. Don was doing all the computer work. I was doing all the filecabinets and other such paperwork. The other three were going through the rest of the boxes and stuff.

Wow! As I sift through these documents I begin too realize that there was at one time some pretty bizarre stuff going on at that Cades Cove underground bunker we had been sent to. Hmm, what's this? Looks almost like a daily log book or a journal of some kind. I'll set this aside and look at it later. Anyhow, according too some of this paperwork, starting late in the Clinton years the government began a black operations program in order too try to discover a way too cloak their military vehicles such as humvees, tanks, transport trucks, etc. and accidently stumbled on not only how too displace time but possibly even how to travel back and forth threw it. However a few years later in order too fund his incursion into Iraq G.W. cut funding to certain programs. Programs that noone outside of those directly involved knew nothing of and as a result they were never able to complete their work. As I explain this to the rest of us I ask "Do you think it's possible that one of the individuals that was involved with this somehow, unofficially continued the work and is somehow behind whats happening too us now?" Don quickly answered with "I suppose it is but it's highly unlikely. Someone would need access to all kinds of crazy things and I wouldn't have a clue as too what." Billy abruptly piped in "There's almost no other logical explanation!" "I guess someone traveling back and forth threw time and purposely changing history would explain a lot." I stated. However Lashawn had the most thought provoking question, "How do we get anyone to believe us, to believe that this is really happening?"

Part V

The Great Bear

What! Again? Where do you keep running off to? Sit down! I'll buy you a beer, no wait, make that two, your gonna need them. Ever since the start of this great novel that your holding in your hands I have been telling you that I'll explain how these time machines work, so here it goes. I'll explain what little I know and understand, if you want too know more you'll have too ask Epitaph yourself and good luck with that, very few individuals know where or should I say when he is and as one of those individuals I ain't saying a thing. Now I'll have you know that I've tried on many occassions too try and get Epitaph too write a book explaining these things, even though it can in know way compare too the fine piece of literature your currently enjoying.

First, what you have are two humongous nuclear powered jet engines. They are forty feet long, fifteen feet wide, fifteen feet high, and there's a forty foot gap between them. They are strapped to the ground by a Tungsten steel frame that runs the entire length and height of each engine both horizontally and vertically. The steel frames punch down many feet into the ground too keep these highly combustible beasts nailed in place. They start off as normal jet engines by sucking in and compressing the air through the spinning compressor wheels at the front. Here's where things get a little different though, the air is now mixed with the fuel. Now this is not regular jet fuel. These particular engines use spiked up rocket fuel. Rocket fuel that has been laced with enriched nuclear material. Once the air and fuel come into contact with each other they ignite, blasting exhaust gasses out the back. There is also rotating turbine wheels in the back of the engine. If it wasn't for the tungsten steel frames these beasts would be scooting along the ground, ripping gouges into mother Earth. One of the turbines spin clockwise while the other spins counter-clockwise. Behind where the fuel and air ignites each engine has two hoppers. This is crucial because at the same time, simultaneously each hopper must recieve one liquid drop. One hopper gets a drop of matter while the other hopper recieves a drop of anti-matter. Now I know some of you mad scientist wanna-be's out there are saying to yourselves "Anti-matter?" "There's no such thing as anti-matter." But trust me there is. Sometime in your future, by orders of Epitaph there are giant manufacturing facilities that artificially produce on huge scales, yep you guessed it, liquid anti-matter. All three elements, the nuclear laced fuel, the drop of matter as well as the drop of anti-matter combine together to create one hell of a source of energy. Most of this energy, before reaching the exhaust part of the engine is sucked up into a tube-like metal vacuum where it meets with the raw energy from the other engine inside a metal box-like energy converter suspended between the two engines. There is a fuse box/electricity conducter attached to the back of this metal energy converter with wires that hook up too what looks like a personal computer, except this by far is not your dads desktop. Someone stationed at this supercomputer will then punch in the necessary information that is required to transport us to whenever. This sends a signal to the energy converter that will then project a massive beam of raw power in the form of a vortex like wormhole, opening the door for us to travel to where-ever we wish. Epitaph has said something about second generation time machines being developed that are supposed too be smaller and easier too operate as well as other things but right now thats all I know about them. Now I know some of you nuclear physicsist and other scientist out there are thinking, Commander Granite, that can't be! Like I said, if you want too know more than go talk to Epitaph. As for me I am currently looking at my new orders and they say that I am to sack mother Russia. Sack mother Russia. Hmm, how come that sounds better than it should.

It is now December of fifteen sixty-four and for the last four years the ruler of Russia, Ivan The Terrible has been living up to that reputation. People of all kinds, especially the Russian aristocracy, the Boyars have been brutalized, beaten, tortured, killed, and anything else imaginable in many different ways. Impaled, boiled alive in tar, liquid metal poured in their ears and mouths and thats just for starters. They should have seen this coming. I mean as a child, just for shits and giggles he would toss cats and dogs out of the Kremlin Tower window just too watch them splatter apart as they hit the ground many meters down from where he was. Now some of the Boyars and other elites have questioned his authority so in a calculating move to gain the support of the people Ivan has decided to abdicate his throne and leave Moscow. He has written a letter to the people of Russia claiming the Boyars and others are stealing from Russia, holding the country back from forward progress in many different ways and that not only do they need too be held accountable but that he as absolute ruler must be allowed to govern as he sees fit. And that includes the punishment of these treasonous individuals. Just as Ivan thought. It doesn't take the people long at all to take to the streets, even in the harsh Russian winter, and demand that Ivan returns and rules with no questions asked. But unbeknownst too the Russian people their new ruler is vastly approaching.

It was almost Feburary of fifteen sixty-five as Ivan and his entourage advance toward the imperial city of Moscow. By now Epitaph troops disguised as both citizens and Russian soldiers have infiltrated the city. Ivan was so confident that he would be back shortly that he left behind what few pieces of artillery his army had. I bet you he's now regretting that mistake. As he and his men got close to the Alexandrovsky Kremlin he finds his own cannons are being used against him. Granted they're not as powerful as the twenty-four pounders I have been using, which I have some of right here with me that are also being used against the Ruskies, but they're doing the job anyhow. They're pea shooters compared too what I have. They're nine to ten centimeters in caliber with a usual range of six hundred meters but since The Kremlin itself sits on a hill overlooking the rest of town I can stretch out a little more of a better range. As the artillary desends down onto the czarist forces men, both alive and dead scatter in all directions. Ivan's infantry falls back, trying to establish a line of defense so that the tsar and others can retreat to safety, like there actually is such a thing when Beelzebub's Boys are involved. The Slavs however are armed with nothing more than matchlock muskets which in no way can compare with the rate of fire and range of my sharpshooters. The ambush is now set. The Epitaph forces, armed with the fg-forty two battle rifle that watched Ivan and his men move threw the city are now springing forth from their places of concealment, encircling the Slavs and callously butchering them to pieces. The Russians don't have a prayer, no matter which god they choose to cry out for. They're being squeezed by Epitaph infantry on all three sides and bombarded by their own cannons from the front. The matchlocks they carry have a rate of fire of three rounds a minute and thats only if all goes well. Our rifles on the other hand average seven to nine hundred rounds per minute and are easily reloaded.

Yes, as you can guess, in the end Russians lie scattered everywhere like rubbish in a field of litter all over the streets of Moscow. Even thou Ivan did everything in his power to escape the carnage him and a few of his royal guards were captured, ALIVE. Little does he know, he is about to recieve a dose of his own medicine. I decided too publicly execute him by a method known as Breaking On The Wheel. He was strapped in his all natural glory to a huge wooden wheel that had many radial spokes. The wheel was then mounted on a colossal size pole that had a hand crank used to slowly revolve the wheel in a giant circle. As the wheel turned, round and round, I used a good size sledge hammer to beat the evil tyrant to a bloody blob and a fleshly mess. The idea is to strike the limbs that are over the gaps between the beams or spokes but I was having way too much fun to care where I struck the madman at. What a adrenaline rush it is too kill someone in such a frenzied way. And it's legal, well at least for me it is.

Now Russia wasn't always the size as you know it too be, so as a result we had too make a few assaults onto the nation at different periods of your history and Ivan The Terrible was only the first stop.

It's a cold, bone chilling November night in seventeen forty-one and for the last fifteen years, ever since the death of Peter The Great the Russian throne has seen more than one ruler. One by one they have all fallen to the wayside one way or another. During this time Elizabeth, one of Peter's daughters has been enjoying her prestigious, socialite status as well as the lusty, sinful night life. Kinda like a renaissance Paris Hilton. But she has now decided that her time too rule has finally arrived. The newest czar to take the throne is a two month old infant which she thinks is a insult to Russia and her family. I can't help but laugh about it. A two month old infant as king of a country, thats a good one. The childs name is Ivan The Sixth and I've been tasked with saving the lad. He will be taken away where he will grow up in the Epitaph world and learn the true way of life. His regent mother on the other hand is to be done away with ASAP.

There is nothing to distinguish us from all the other Russian guards that are patrolling the palace. Except we aren't Russians and we know that the sparks are about too be ignited and the fireworks are going to fly. We're walking around The Peterhof, the palace that Peter The Great had built when in seventeen-twelve he named Saint Petersburg as the new Russian capital. If your ever on vacation I recomend you pay this place a visit. It has so many rooms you could spend days just wandering around from one to the other. And thats just the inside. The grounds this place sits on are even bigger with it's many fountains and golden statues as well as patches of trees that dot the place here and there. It's just so beautiful that it takes your breath away and leaves you longing for a place like this of your own. But tonight there is no enjoying the scenery. Elizabeth and her cohorts plan too just simply walk right in and execute a bloodless coup d'etat. It's actually a good plan since it's not uncommon at all too see her here at the palace during anytime of the day or night. Here they come now so get ready. In fact you might wanna go and hide.

We let them tie up their horses and walk halfway across the courtyard before we surprised her and her friends with our gunfire. There was no need for the Fg-Forty-two this time but I still wanted some rapid-fire capability. Tonight we're going with the Nineteen-O-Three Springfield Rifle. It uses a thirty caliber projectile that can fly at about twenty-eight hundred feet per second as it sails out the opened end of the twenty-four inch barrel. I bet a lot of you gun enthusiast out there would love to shoot this fine bolt action piece of wood and metal. Well guess what? Your wrong, we're not using the bolt action version, we've got a nifty little thing called The Pedersen Device. This device fits into a slot on the side of the rifle and it turns the already deadly bolt action Springfield into a fully functional forty-round, semi-automatic rifle which in World War One is a top secret project of the American Government. The Pedersen Device is a invention of John Pedersen, a employee of Remington Arms who is concerned about troops entering The Great War and their lack of firepower while on the move. Though a good idea at the time it will never see battle action because of the war's end.

Oh. Wait a minute. They're seeing battle action right now. The queen want-to-be and her companions are face down on the ground trying to hide behind trees, bushes, statues, anything. Of course they're dumb-founded as they've never encountered anything like this before. They thought they had everything under control by bringing their flintlock muskets with them just in case but now they know their in over their head. I mean look at the bullets fly over their heads. They're sticking low to the ground as they try to retreat back to their horses. Silly Russians. Me and my men simultaneously hurl World War Two American Pineapple style grenades at the princess and her posse. The deafening explosions was enough for them to reconsider this little adventure of theirs. Those who survived and could actually manage got up to get back to their horses and the hell away from this place but as the grenades sent shrapnel flying everywhere me and my men were already pursuing them all, stopping only to shoot a fleeing target.

Not many of the Rus' made it to their waiting steeds. They fell as numberless victims to either grenade shrapnel or Springfield shells. However Elizabeth was among those few who thought they were gonna make it as they galloped toward hopeful safety. Safety they hoped to achieve by putting as much distance between themselves and The Peterhof Palace as possible. Like thats really gonna help them. Once again I called upon The Riding Reapers. You know, those fellows who sliced and diced the Huns while on motorcycles and sidecars. As the Russian throne usurpers try to dash out of dangers way their horses soon become spooked as the deafening, mechanical roar of our BMW R Seventy-five Motorbikes come upon them all from behind. It would be as if The Hells Angels were chasing you down main street while you are on a bicycle, oh wait that would be us as well chasing you down main street. As our booming, blaring, bikes shorten the gap between us and our prey the troops who get to ride in the sidecars and pretend that they're in The Isle Of Man now raise and level the firearm of choice. The Beaumont-Adams Russian Model Eighteen Fifty-five. Yes, I know, the irony of it all. Using a Russian gun against Russians but you gotta love it. We're using the eleven point two millimeter version. It's a five shot revolver with a fine feeling walnut grip. It's double action with a fixed sight on the end of the five inch barrel. It weighs thirty ounces and it's over-all length is between eleven and twelve inches. It was produced by The London Armoury Company until eighteen sixty-five. As the sidecar shootist squeeze their triggers and let the lead fly not only are Russians dropping from their saddles with bone crunching momentum but the gap between us and them continues to shrink evermore. While dodging dead and damaged Russians who have suddenly found themselves on the ground without their horses beneath them we pull out the ropes and rudely lasso those few remaining freedom seeking escapees. What were they thinking? Escape. Most of them were gutted on the spot. Left to die in the cold, frigid, Russian weather but the princess, I have special plans for her, cruel plans for her. Elizabeth is ruthlessly forced back towards town where her sinister execution will immediately take place. This spectacle proceeds infront of all who come to bare witness and actually draws a good size crowd since Elizabeth was a nationally renowned celebrity.

First she is stripped to her natural nakedness. Her clothing left laying at her feet as she's shoved into the wooden chair I had brought forth. Two taped together golf balls are rammed into her mouth followed up by having her mouth then duct taped shut. Now her screams will be mere whimpers and screaming, I mean whimpering she will be doing. Her fingers are forced into pilliwinks, thats fingerscrews for you non-articulate individuals. Fingerscrews are metal bars that are held together by long threaded screws. The interior surface of the metal bars has sharp metal points protruding out from them for added, extra pain. As if your fingers being slowly crushed when the hand crank is turned wasn't enough. I bet you she wishes she could loudly scream right now, he, he. But my fun is only starting. I now pull the pliers out of the red hot fire and place them on her oh so sensitive nipples. Her breasts shoved in my face as she arches her back in excruciating pain. If she could speak she would probably be begging me too stop, but why do that when I'm having so much fun. Next I decided that since she liked too have that thing of hers bored out I'll give her a reaming like she's never had before. No I'm not going too sex-a-cute her, get your mind out of the gutter, she would actually like that. Instead out of my bag of naughty toys I'm going to bring forth a pear and that doesn't mean I'm going to spit fruit on her either. The Pear Of Anguish as it was often referred too as is a bronze torture device in the shape of, yep you guessed it, a pear. First I brutally jam this torture toy straight into her vagina as far as I can. Then by turning the handle on top, the central screw thread slowly pushes open the spoon-like leaves. As the leaves spread apart from each other, stretching her vaginal walls far wider than they ever have before. The small, metal spikes on the end of the leaves are exposed. Ripping and tearing her innards so that she may slowly bleed. My fun is not at a end yet. I grab a utility knife and make little itty, bitty, tiny, paper-like cuts all over her body. After cutting open the lemons before her I slowly squeeze them, straight onto the tiny cuts I've just carved upon her. Once again her body twists and turns with pain, thrusting her chest towards me. Hey, can someone hand me the salt. Finally, and this is the messiest part, I take a state-of-the-art surgical knife and leisurely carve the skin right off of her body exposing everything beneath. Muscle, tissue, everything so that now she looks like a living blob of human-like jelly. She'll eventually die though it will take awhile. I leave her to rot as I slowly walk away. I leave many guards posted too hold back the enthralled, grossed-out crowd. They can watch her suffer from where they are but I don't want them to get anywhere near her.

After the way I treated Elizabeth you probably think I hate women but thats not so, just treacherous, treasonous ones. In fact I'm trying too save one right now. We've been locked up in my personal quarters now for all night long. We've froliced and fornicated everywhere in my room. We started on the bed but have somehow ended up on the floor rolling all over the bearskin rugs that lay all about my chambers. We're now just cuddled up enjoying each others embrace as we bake by the fireplace. Yes, we're a little close to the fire but the sweat that pours off of us has nothing to do with the flames, unless you count the flame of passion between us. I was ordered to sack mother Russia and I must proudly say I have. Hey, I don't want Epitaph too get mad at me. I'm just doing as he says. The woman I've been rompping with will someday be the face and personification of mother Russia but in order to see that she lives too see that day I had no choice but to impregnate her so that she can deliver what people believe too be a heir to the throne. It's her duty. Her only duty. And believe it or not her royal husband is not in the least bit intrested in her or sex with any other woman for that matter. Yes, he's a overgrown, immature child who wouldn't know what too do with it even if he had a instruction manual, which is where I come in. Even though her husband is not yet king he could have her locked up or worse for not producing a child. He must think these things happen by spontaneous conception or something, I don't know, but the poor princess was in fear of her life, and rightfully so. It took me a few years to pull this off and I had many cohorts, all of them female. We took up residence at The Peterhof. I had assumed the alias of Sergei Saltykov and I am in charge of keeping things tidy. Yes, I'm a glorified maid, but I'm the head maid damn-it so leave me alone. Besides it's for the cause. Anyway the princess who was born Sophie Friederike Auguste in Stettin, Germany was summoned to Russia in seventeen forty-four at the ripe young age of fifteen. Upon her arrival she was baptized and christened as Catherine. At first she was joyous and giddy and full of high hopes of all that Russia had too offer but after eight years of a dull, sex-less, non-romantic marriage she was at her wits-end, almost ready too throw in the towel. During those mundane years my accomplices kept the pressure up by bending her ear. As more and more the royal family that she married into started to look down upon her the easier it became for my female assistants too convince her not only of what she needed to do but that it is the right thing to do. Which gets me where I am right now. Laying by the fire on a bearskin rug in the arms of Catherine The Great. Of course she's not great yet and she thought me silly when I told her of things yet to come. Thinking I was just fantasizing as I foretold her future to her. That she will take the throne in seventeen sixty-two. Expand the boundaries of Russia. Put down peasant revolts left and right. Modernize Russian government as well as many other glorious acts, but unfortunately my time here is almost through. So if you don't mind I think I'm going to turn the lights out now and hit it one last time.

Something else that is almost through in Russia is czarist rule and of course I have too change that. At twenty-six years of age Nicholas Alexandrovich Romanov The Second had ascended the throne in eighteen ninety-four. Almost immediately his rule was overshadowed by bad omens. For example on the day of his coronation he held a enormous party in a monstrously, oversized field just outside of Moscow. People of all walks of life, from peasants to boyars attended this festivity and all was well until the food and drinks ran out. This caused widespread pandemonium and thousands of people lost their lives by being trampled on by the overzealous crowd. By this time however the five foot six czar had already moved on to a different location and when it became known that he was off jubilantly partying somewhere else while his subjects were dying well, it just didn't look good. Starting at the turn of the century social and economic unrest was plaguing the country in many forms. Factory workers were striking, teachers were striking, peasant farmers revolting, and revolutionists were creating many forms of domestic terrorism. So what did the blue-eyed, brown haired czar do? Get the country in a war. He tried to annex Manchuria and Korea, but the budding, oriental power of Japan saw this as a threat and pushed back. This all broke out into The Russo-Japanese war in nineteen-o-four. A year later after suffering many humiliating defeats on both land and sea Russia was forced too surrender. The bad war just enticed the populace all the more. In January of nineteen-o-five when unarmed, peaceful demonstrators marched to the capital building too present Nicholas with a petition of what they needed the royal guards opened fire and gunned them down like ducks on a pond. From this moment forth the country was a tinderbox waiting too blow. Workers strikes became more frequent, peasant unrest is at a all time high, revolutionist terrorism reaches a fever-pitch, and if your the czar there's worse yet, military mutinies. There was many attempts on Nicholas's life and this madness will continue until The Great War breaks out in nineteen-fourteen. It doesn't take Russia long to find itself on the recieving end of the war and in nineteen-fifteen Nicholas takes direct control of the armed forces. As the war continues to go bad for Russia this just makes the tsar, in the eyes of the people look all the more at fault for everything that goes wrong. The poor guy just can't win for losing now can he. Nicholas makes his way to the front lines too take a personal gander at the troops. Even though he's a cool, calm, collective, low-tempered individual he's also indecisive and not much for chit-chat. In fact if you didn't know any better you would never guess that your face to face with the Emperor Of Russia. Of course the troops kinda saw this as a sign of weak leadership and this drove morale from poor to non-existent. While still at the frontlines when, in late Feburary of nineteen-seventeen he recieved word that Saint Petersburg had erupted in violent riots and that the rioters included police as well as military troops he went to hop aboard his personal train to get home and see too his family's safety. He never even made it to the train. He was stopped by Epitaph troops disguised as Russian peasants. I personally informed him that to step on that train is too seal his fate and the fate of everyone he cares for.

So here I am now. Sitting on the Royal Train that has been halted just south of Saint Petersburg by angry and violent protesters. The train itself is ten carriages long. That's not counting the steam engine and fuel car directly behind it. Now I know that most of you understand just how locomotive steam engines work but I'll explain it anyway for all the dunderheads out there, and you know who you are. Oh, wait a minute. You probably don't, because your a dunderhead. First the individual operating the train throws fuel into the firebox, in this case it's wood. The gases that arise as a result of the burning wood are drawn into the boiler threw long tubes. The water contained in the boiler with help from airflow in the smoke stack is then heated up. Steam is now traveling to the steam-dome which is where the throttle body is located. This controls power to the pistons. Once inside the cylinder the steam pushes the pistons back and this will put the main rod into action. The main rod pushes the crank pin and this is what causes the wheels of the train to start moving. The steam now makes its way to the backside of the piston and pushes it forward too start the cycle again. While all this is happening flue gases in the form of spent steam is blown out the smoke stack. Now I don't expect many of you, regardless of your I.Q. too know that flue gases are almost any type of gas that enters the atmosphere as a result of being the product of a fireplace, furnace, waterheater, or in this case a boiler.

Now I must say, this is actually a pretty nice train the czar has. There's a sleeping car, a kitchen car, even one for the children, which he had five of. There's also one for all their luggage as well as their servants, and one for all the railroad servicemen that might be needed if the trip went disastrous. Believe it or not, there is also a train-car with a bath-tub in it. How convenient. My favorite one however is the saloon car. Yep, that's where I've spent most of my time so far. May as well enjoy myself if I have too be here. All ten carriages on the outside have been painted a bright blue. On the inside however the Indian Teak floors are covered with high fassion carpets of all kinds. Those that haven't been covered with carpets are layered with linoleum. The furniture is made of various woods. Red beech and Satinwood. Polished Oak, Walnut, White and Gray beech. There's also Maple and Karelian birch. Some of the walls have been upholstered in leather as well as many different colors of silk. Family photographs and Tsarist icons are proudly displayed all over the walls. Now the walls in the saloon car are green silk which highlights the soft, mahogany furniture. The plush carpet has a checkered design. There are porcelain and glass vases everywhere. And a ash-tray of red stone and Dutch porcelain.

Part of the mob that's outside of this beautiful train are members of a legislative body known as The Duma. They were briefly given some political power back in late nineteen-o-five. However in early o-six they pushed their luck and asked for more than the czar was willing too give. As you can guess, he took their powers away faster than he gave them. They stayed in contact with each other and now here it is, eleven years later. They are now demanding far more of the tsar than he ever would have dreamed of giving them. Thinking that I am Nicholas and that they have him trapped, for the last eight days they have been giving written messages to the czar's guards. At least that's what they think. Of course the Tsar's guards are actually my guards and they're Epitaph infantry. Since I've been stuck here on this train for so long now I'm starting to grow tired of this. I wish Epitaph would hurry up with those new time machines so I could just zap in and out of everywhere at whatever time I want. Oh well, hopefully they'll be ready by the time the next book is released. They have now handed Nicholas, I mean me a final ultimatum. They demand full abdication of the throne by the tsar and nothing less. Okay, I guess it's time too quit playing games. I sent their leader, Michael Rodzianko my one word reply. Nope. He probably had just recieved my word when I gave orders for the madness too begin. I and my troops lowered the train windows overlooking the bundled up assembly that made the horded up mob. I also had men whipping open the carriage side doors. During these last eight days I had openings cut into the roof of each train car where I now had more men poking up at while they too looked down upon the crowd. I hate too waste good whiskey but I couldn't resist tossing a molotov cocktail into the herd of Russians before we all opened fire with the M Nineteen Forty-one light machine gun which is a American made, recoil-operated firearm. It uses a thirty zero six springfield cartridge. It's forty-two inches long and weighs about thirteen pounds. It's designed in the late nineteen thirties. It has a twenty-five round curved, single column magazine attached to the left side of the receiver. It also has a wooden stock and can fire two to six hundred rounds per minute. As the bodies hit the ground like branches being cut from trees the crowded together populace dispersed like bugs in the dark after a light has been flicked on. They are wildly bolting in all directions. Like that can help them. Like they have a safe place to run to. I have called in one of the first bomber planes known to mankind. Actually I called in ten of them but who's counting. It's a two seat, funny looking biplane that kinda looks like a baby carriage with a light, steel, extended frame trailing behind it. It will serve many purposes in World War One as soon as the war breaks out. Reconnaissance, artillery spotting, ground attacking, day and night bombing, etc..., but I want it just for it's bombs. The Voisin Three can carry loads of two to three hundred pounds of bombs and will actually have successful day and night raids deep into Germany. With it's single one hundred and twenty horsepower Salmson M-Nine engine and speeds up to sixty-five miles per hour the thirty-one foot long planes are now flying over the fleeing mass of Russian nationalist. Bombs away!I watch Russian bodies burst into pieces from the falling bombs as I continue too mow them down with my gun. The blood and guts flying high into the air before landing and soaking into the now drenched Earth. The madness ensuing as those few that have so far survived not only push and shove each other to the ground in a invain attempt to escape but they also stomp on, run over, and leap over bodies in their path of flight. Bodies that are both alive and dead. The Voisin Three's continue to buzz by dropping their explosive devices before fading into the distant horizon.

All is silent now. Czarist opposition forces have been completely decimated, never to arise again. Not unless they figure out how to go Resident Evil on my ass and rise as flesh eating zombies. Other than that my work is done. Nicholas has been safely returned to power. I gave him certain instructions on how too keep his throne safe from anymore would-be usurpers as well as who to give power too when the time comes. He knew as well as I did that it couldn't be his heir.

Part VI

A Forecast Of War!

Hey now! Before you even think about getting up and going somewhere you just sit right back down. We're not done here yet.

As for this next mission I didn't personally participate. This was something Epitaph says needs too be handled by him. That the individual he's going to see is a sly, shifty little bastard who is not too be trusted at all. No matter what!

Downtown Vienna, Austria Nineteen-o-seven

It's a chilly November night in the capital city of the Austro-Hungarian Empire. You can almost feel the wind in your bones as it blows debris by you. The wind stinging your face as it noisily rattles the street signs you pass.

At least thats how it seemed to the five foot nine inch tall, eighteen year old young man before he stepped into his little, roach infested apartment on Stubengasse Strasse. Placing his fine handled ivory cane by the door as he walked into the darkened, dreary place. He fumbled around in the dark trying too light candles and oil lamps in a attempt to illuminate the dull, colorless room. Outside of the lamps and candles it didn't have much. No wall decorations or pictures of anykind. Just a couple of rough, raggedy looking chairs that by my guess are very uncomfortable. He was lost in the realms of his own mind when the calm voice rudely pierced his thoughts. "Mister Schicklgruber." The young man abruptly turned toward the source of his verbal assailant. His fierce blue eyes scanning the room. "Who are you and where have you ever heard that name from?" "Don't you ever call me that again!" The man was practically yelling as he strode across the room trying too reach his cane. "And what are you going too do with that Adolf, hit me?" By now the young man was flabbergasted. Who was this stranger? "Do you believe in myths and legends Adolf?" Holding his cane he now also grabbed one of the oil lamps and held it before him to get a look at the stranger before him. He also gave the smart ass reply of "Maybe I do and maybe I don't." "Why would you ask such a thing?" Adolf riposted. "Cause thats what I am, a myth, a legend. Surely you've heard of me, Lord Epitaph." Adolf was about to make some other wise guy reply when Epitaph, dressed in his holy robes stepped from the shadows of the small room. One look at my mysterious master and Adolf knew that he better mind his p's and q's. "Now that I have your attention, sit down Mister Hitler." Adolf Hitler walked to the chair and did as he was told. Epitaph walked over to the other chair and pulled it across the room before taking a seat himself. Now he can look this man in the eyes, face to face. Epitaph started with "I know why your here. To get in the school of art. Your not going to get in. I have plans for you. Plans for your life. As long as you do what I say, when I say everything will be just fine. But the moment you betray me, the moment you break your word to me everything that can go wrong will go wrong. Everything that can go bad for you will go bad for you. For the next few years your life is going too be hard. Starting next month when your mother passes away. In the next few months you'll come back to Vienna. You'll be okay for the next year but starting in nineteen-o-nine you'll find yourself homeless. A wandering vagabond sleeping on park benches and in abandoned buildings." "What?" The young Adolf interrupted. "Don't worry. These things must happen. You'll learn many lessons about life that will serve you well later on. In nineteen thirteen, even though your still homeless I want you to go to Munich." "In the fatherland?" The young Hitler excitably asked. Even at this youthful age he felt more loyalty towards Germany than his native Austria. "Yes, the fatherland. Here's where things are going too start to turn for you. As soon as The Great War breaks out in nineteen-fourteen you are too enlist in the German army. You'll be assigned to the first company of the Sixteenth Bavarian Reserve Infantry Regiment." "The Great War, Germany's going too win The Great War?" The wild eyed Hitler asked. "No. Germany's going to lose this war." The look on the young Hitler's face said it all. He was shocked and appalled. Germany was going too lose the war! "Don't worry, not only will this war last two years twice." Hitler interrupted again with "Wouldn't that be four years?" Epitaph just looked at him. "Yes, the war will last four years. Once again you will learn many lessons that will serve you well later on in life. You'll also recieve many medals for bravery and honor including the Iron Cross other wise known as the Aryan Cross." Epitaph knew what the word Aryan insinuated to the young German nationalist. "Unfortunately in about a century from now a American motorcycle company known as West Coast Choppers will adopt this symbol of purity and it will be sported around by all sorts of inferior humans." Once again, the look on Hitler's face said it all. "I've already told you that Germany will not win, what I haven't told you is why. The war doesn't end because the German army is defeated. It ends because of criminals within the fatherland who betray Germany. When the time is right you'll know who they are." "About a year after the war I want you too join a fledgling political group known as The German Workers Party. You'll quickly rise through the ranks to the top position. Also shortly after the war there is a chap who will bust onto the international stage because of the movies he makes. He will go by the name of Charlie Chaplin. Now you will not meet him personally but when he arrives I want you too start wearing the same style of mustache as him. It will take you far in your political career." "In nineteen twenty-three you'll get the bright idea to take the country by force. Even though it fails try it anyhow. Not only will you learn more lessons from this but it will give you time too write your book. Trust me, THIS book will sell like hotcakes." "Now when you get out of jail you'll be banned from giving speeches until nineteen twenty-seven. From nineteen twenty-seven on give as many public speeches as possible. In nineteen thirty-three you will become master of Germany. You will rule peacefully until you forcibly annex land from Poland. Land that is stripped from Germany at the end of The Great War. This annexation of Poland will start a second great war. During this second war almost all the world will gang-up on you and Germany. Your biggest threat will be The Land Of Europes Most Racially Fit, don't worry when the time is right I will take care of them. Another thing is that you will be tempted to invade Russia. I'm telling you right now, don't do it! I'm stressing, don't do it!" Even as he spoke it, Epitaph already knew that the future German leader was going too do it. He was going to invade Russia anyhow. Epitaph continued with "As long as you obey and follow my directions I will make you the sledge hammer of history." As Epitaph got up from his seat he looked down at the future German leader. "During the course of your life, from time to time, I will visit you." Then Epitaph simply turned and walked away. Except he didn't exit threw the door, it appeared as if he went right threw the wall. Damn-it, he must be using a prototype of one of those new time machines. I wish he would let me have one. The young Adolf Hitler was just left sitting there. He was already overwhelmed with all he had been told but when Epitaph walked threw the wall he now knew that the Demon Of Death was by far no myth.

Part VII

Spread The Word

We have been sitting in that nice, plush hotel room in Southern Virginia for the last few days, none of us sure about what too do when Don recieved a phone call from a old colleague. A colleague who is still with the C.I.A. Somehow, despite all the weird happenings this man still remembered Don and was just curious as too where he was and what he's been doing. Don asked the guy, I guess his name is Ryan Reynolds if he could meet us in Bristol, Tennessee.

A few days later at a little ma and pa style restaurant in Bristol we all took a seat at the only over sized table they had. Me, Don, Lashawn, Billy, and Running Dog were met by Ryan and his associates. Ryan's actually a good looking man. Sss, kinda hot. Standing at about five eleven he's in his mid-thirties with brownish, blond hair and sparkling green eyes. His clean shaven baby face is ruggedly chiseled with a rough finish. His partner is a woman in her late twenties. Finally! Someone I can have some girl talk with. She's about five nine with brown eyes and dirty blond hair that hangs past her shoulders. The tips dangling about where her breasts are. For all you guys out there she has long, firm, strong looking legs and pouty, red lips. Her name is Sarah Western and I hope too get to know her better. Don't get me wrong, I like the guys and everything but sometimes a woman just needs another chick to chat with. Accompanying them are two guards. Yes, they're both guys. They're both tall black men. I think their names are Jason Worley and Alfred Jackson.

After the petite waitress took our orders we all just kinda made small talk with each other for awhile till eventually Don got down to business and started telling Ryan about all the strange things that have been happening. You know, few people actually knowing who we are. Not being known at our jobs. Friends and relatives having no clue who we are and the appearance of the unknown, to us unheard of Epitaph Empire. Even though Ryan was skeptical, only because he had five people swearing too these events, he swore up and down that the Epitaph Empire has existed for over fifteen hundred years. We all told him that it's not possible but him and the three with him kept arguing otherwise. Before things got too far out of control Don said to everyone "Why don't all of us just go to that bunker at Cades Cove and you can see for yourselves some of the stuff thats down there. We're only a few hours away from the place so it's not like it's that far out of the way." It took a little more persuading but we finally got Ryan and his gang too come along with us back to the Cades Cove bunker.

We had all been holed-up down there for a few days now. Ryan and his cohorts were amazed by some of the stuff that had been left behind by the original occupants that labored here. He was convinced that some pretty shady things must have at one time been going on here but too him it was still a big leap between governmental shady business and some madman running amok threw time and history. Speaking of history I happened to find, of all things a genuine history book and as I handed it to Ryan I said to him, kind of angerly "Here, this is what the true history of the world is!" Now before I handed that book to Ryan I flipped threw it just too make sure it was the actual history that you and I know too be real but I didn't start thinking about it until later. How is it that history book was not effected by whatever's going on. How and why is it that nothing in this bunker is effected but the rest of the world is. There must be a reason why and I bet you Epitaph knows that answer. Which means whoever Epitaph is crazy he may be, stupid he is not. It makes me wonder if he plans on coming back here someday?

Ryan and his group thoroughly paged through the thick history book and of course nowhere in there did they find anything about Epitaph or his empire. Finally he looked up at us and with a odd look upon his face he spoke. "Well, I'm sure something strange is going on but I'm not sure as too what. There's a lot of things here I just don't understand." He continued with "Since it's kinda late me, Sarah, and the guards will wait until morning to head back towards D.C. I'll look into this but I can't guarantee you I'll find anything, either way I'll let you know something." Don said thats okay and that we too will head out in the morning and that we will be eagerly waiting too hear from him.

A few days later as Ryan and his friends were cruising along on their way back towards Washington D.C. curious about everything we had just told them about and hoping, just hoping that while back in D.C. they could find out something new. They were in for a shock when approximately ten miles outside of the city they came upon the suited up guards and were forced to stop. At first they were asked to turn around when Ryan flashed his i.d. showing him too be a high ranking member in the C.I.A. "Sorry sir." The guard replied through his gas mask. "But unless you have the proper gear on I still have to ask you to turn around." "What's this all about, what's happening here?" Ryan asked. "I'm just trying to get back to headquarters than hopefully home." The guard just stood there for a moment, kinda like he was speechless but then he finally said. "Headquarters?" "Home?" "What are you talking about, ain't noone lived here in sixty-six years." Now it was Ryan and the rest of the crew that was speechless. "What are you talking about, I was just here two weeks ago." You could almost hear the confusion in Ryans voice as it started to get louder. "Sir, it's like I just said, ain't noone lived here in the last sixty-six years. The radiation levels are still too high." Everybody kinda just looked at each other for awhile until Ryan finally told the guard, "Okay, we're gonna just go ahead and turn around then, have a good day." As they all headed back down the road to, well I don't think they know where they're going but one thing is for sure that they do know. The world they left behind when they stepped down into that bunker and the one they stepped out into are two vastly different worlds. Two worlds that are nothing alike. Another thing they now know for sure, Epitaph has struck again.

Part VIII

End Of The Allies

That's it! I don't know where it is you keep running off to but if you get up just one more time I'm going to tie your damn ass to that chair! Now sit down and pay attention, oh I forgot you can't. Your so broke your reality check would bounce.

Everything that Epitaph had told the young Hitler on that fateful night in the dictators apartment had come to be. The Great War, Germany's defeat, his stint in jail, his rise to power, everything. And just as Epitaph predicted, in the summer of nineteen forty-one Hitler invaded Russia. Once again, just as Epitaph told the German leader "... the moment you break your word to me everything that can go wrong will go wrong...", and ever since he invaded Russia everything has been going wrong for both Hitler and Germany. That was three and a half years ago, it's now December of nineteen forty-four and Germany's been getting it's butt kicked all over Europe. Armies are closing in on the fatherland from both sides, east and west. Not that it's south flank is doing any better.

However Hitler is about too change all this. He knows that the Western Allies believe his armies are incapable of anything except retreating and that on the borders of Germany they have just settled down for a long winters nap.

Yeah, it's true that the Allies have been beating the Nazi's back all across Europe for the last six months with very few problems and little opposition. So much to the point that they're halting all operations more because they outran their supply lines than the encrouching winter weather. With the snow coming down and the temperatures dropping below freezing who in their right mind wants too be fighting anyhow?

One thing is for sure noone, not even Epitaph has ever accused Hitler of being in his right mind. So in the wee hours of December sixteenth, with the wet, rain-like snow still falling and the temperatures still below freezing it was a complete shock and surprise too the Western Allies when they found themselves being bombarded by artillery in the opening moments of what Hitler called "Watch On The Rhine."

It was around five thirty A.M. when the Germans started the artillery barrage that would last almost two hours. Almost two thousand artillery guns roared to life at this moment in time and all the Western Allies could do was hunker down in their snow filled holes and hope for the best. The ground all around them exploding as it was struck with shells, throwing dirt, debris, and snow high into the air. Trees all around them falling like toothpicks that have just dropped from your hand. Grown men screaming after being struck by whole shells and flying shrapnel and thats only if they had time to scream before they died. If you were one of these soldiers the cry of "Medic!" was heard all around you. So much so that it sounded like a echo.

When the two hundred and fifty thousand plus German soldiers charged forward along a sixty-to eighty mile front, with over two thousand tanks they greatly outnumbered their opponents. I have no idea how much other equipment they had but I know they had for sure self-propelled cannons, half-tracks, and transport trucks but none of this would do them any good.

For a little over a week the Nazi's had the Allies reeling back as they dished out one ass-whipping after another, taking towns left and right, leaving a brutal path of destruction behind them as they marched on. This would all come to a stop however as they had very little fuel to start with and they were beginning to run out. Hitler's plan relied on the Germans resupplying themselves by capturing Allie depots which was a far stretch as is but what do you expect from someone who's not in their right mind. The Germans did manage to capture some fuel here and there but nowhere near the amounts that they needed to continue their push. After about eight to nine days of fighting in thick, knee-deep snow and dark, cloudy skies the Allies had somehow managed to regroup and hold onto key towns, Bastogne being the most important.

Conditions for the Allie soldiers in Bastogne are bad and about to get worse. No winter clothes, very low ammo supplies, small amounts of military equipment, next to no food, you name it, it's pretty bad. Ever since December twentith they have been completely surrounded by the German Fifth Panzer Army as well as the Forty-seventh Panzer Corps. All roads leading into and out of Bastogne were completely cut off to Allied armies. Intense fighting between the two had been taking place on a daily basis. All around you the snap, crackle, bang of machine gun fire reports the current conditions of your fellow soldiers. However ever since the Allies stabilized the situation they have now diverted troops to the aid and relief of the beleaguered One Hundred And First Airbourne Division that has been doggedly defending Bastogne. They have called in troops from the north and south to help with the situation.

Christmas Eve, Nineteen Forty-Four:

As of yet the back-up forces have not made it to Bastogne and their not going to make it, he he, ha ha. I am currently about thirty thousand feet in the air as I sit in the seat operating the weapons system of a Tu Twenty-two M Tupolev. Yes, this is a Russian bomber from the nineteen seventies but we've taken the liberties of painting it up to look just like a bonafide Nazi aircraft complete with a swastika on the tail fin. It's about one hundred and forty feet long and stands about thirty-six feet high. It weighs well over one hundred thousand pounds and can reach speeds exceeding one thousand, two hundred miles per hour. Even though we're only thirty thousand feet above Bastogne we, if need be could probably go another ten to fifteen thousand feet higher and we can get there at a rate of ninty-one feet per second. Now there are three other people in this plane with me. The pilot, co-pilot, and navigator. Our mission is to bomb to bits Bastogne, all roads leading in and out, any and all relief armies on their way to Bastogne and the rest of Belgium that is not currently under Nazi control. As I press the buttons to drop the free falling bombs I can't help but be in a joyous mood and I have the rest of the crew helping me too sing my own rendition of 'Deck The Halls' which goes a little something like this. "Deck the halls with bombs and bullets fla, la, la, la, la la, la, la, la tis the season to be gory fla, la, la, la, la la, la, la, la..." come on and join in, I'll teach you the words. Anyhow, bombs away and merry christmas Western Allies from your good friends Epitaph and Caesarion.

Now the Nazi forces on the ground just kind of assumed that Hitler had been the one who ordered the night-time air raid and as it helped their situation they really didn't put much thought into it before they launched their massive, all-out attack on christmas day. Now before they somehow messed this up and turned it into a complete debacle I already had Epitaph Infantry Troops stationed on the ground that looked just like true Nazi soldiers in every way. Ya, they have on the latest in state of the art kevlar body armor and other personal protective gear but overtop of all this they wear true Nazi uniforms. The only major difference there is, is that my troops are carrying the M-Fourteen rifle. This is a automatic rifle that fires seven point sixty-two by fifty-one millimeter shells and will be put in service in nineteen fifty-seven. It weighs eleven and a half pounds and is forty-six and-a-half inches long. It shoots between seven hundred and seven hundred fifty rounds per minute. It also has a effective range of about five hundred yards with a twenty round detachable box magazine. My men also have with them a enormous number of true Nazi tanks. How many tanks do we have with us? Let's just say we have so many tanks we could actually run right over each and every Allie soldier and still have tanks bringing up the rear. And that's just tanks, that's not counting our self-propelled guns, Flak eighty-eights, mortar launchers and whatever else we have with us. But anywho, we have two different kinds of Nazi tanks. The ones that are out front, spearheading this attack are the Neubaufahrzeug. These are medium tanks that are six point six meters long, two point nineteen meters wide and almost three meters tall with a six man crew. The turret does turn three hundred and sixty degrees but it has too be done manually. It has two hundred and fifty horse-power with seven gears. Six forward and one reverse. It can reach speeds of thirty kilometers per hour. Now we did have too beef up it's armor as it's standard dimensions were a little under par, but that's okay, we fixed it. Now the second tank we're using is the real powerhouse. Even though they're playing the supporting role they are the brawn of everything. This is the super heavy Maus Tank. With it's one hundred and five meter long barrel and a length of just over ten meters it weighs just a tad over one hundred and eighty-five thousand kilograms. It's width and height are a little under four meters. once again the turret rotates three hundred and sixty degrees. It has a MB Five Hundred Seventeen Diesel Engine except it only has four gears, two forward and two backwards. It's tracks are one hundred and ten centimeters wide and it's armor didn't need doctored up in any way.

When the Nazi's launched their attack we were right there with them. They were so consumed with the mission before them that they didn't notice us, much. However with our help they managed to break threw and take Bastogne. Like the Allies actually had a chance with us there. For the next few months both real Nazi's and Epitaph troops disguised as Nazi's beat the Western Allies back across The English Channel reclaiming all the lost territory. France, Belgium, Luxembourg, everything. All of Fortress Europe is once again under Nazi rule.

Upon hearing that the Western Allies had been defeated Hitler, for awhile was very jubilant but his happiness didn't last for long. He still has the Russians closing in from the east and since it was late March before he was able to transfer his Western forces to the otherside the Russians were still able to make their way to Berlin. They have been constantly bombarding the city which now lays in ruins. They're trying to take the city block by block, street by street, and they're closing in on The Reichs Chancellery which is where Hitler is or should I say under. His underground bunker lays almost fifty feet below the grounds surface and it's concrete shell is about four meters thick. As the Russian assault continues heavy flakes of concrete dust fill the ventilation system and sprinkle into the rooms of this underground liar. The halls of this place are dark and narrow. The rooms themselves, which there is somewhere between twenty and thirty are nothing more than small, cramped quarters and weren't ever really ment to be lived in, but Hitler and his staff have been here for almost three months now.

April Thirtieth, Hitler's Underground Bunker:

It was just the day before that Hitler married his long time mistress Eva Braun. However with the Russians closing in he wasn't sure if there was any hope in sight or not. This all played heavily on his mind as he and Eva shuffled their way to his private chambers. However his mind was abruptly wiped clean as soon as they both stepped into his room. Sitting on his couch was a figure he had not seen in a long time. "Lord Epitaph!" The words had barely fallen from his lips when Epitaph's guards had grabbed him from behind. Two took a-hold of him while two grabbed Eva. There was also two others that just stood present with some kind of assault rifle in their hands. "What's with this, what's this all about?" The dictator was shouting as Epitaph stood up, raising a single finger to his lips in a shush gesture. He slowly walked towards Hitler at a lackadaisical, deliberate, methodical pace before stopping directly in front of him, now face to face. "What did I tell you Adolf?" The dictator just stood silent, not sure of what to say or do. "The moment you break your word to me all that can go wrong for you will go wrong for you. I also told you not to invade Russia and what did you do, you invaded anyhow. Just look at Germany, look at everything, all this because of your betrayal, now I have to clean this mess up too!" Epitaph was practically yelling. "What do you mean clean this..." The words weren't even out of the dictators mouth when Epitaph interrupted him. "What, you actually think it was your forces that saved the west, that Watch On The Rhine was actually going to work. It worked because my troops were there, it was my troops that saved Western Europe!" Hitler just stood silent, his mouth slightly ajar as Epitaph continued. "Now I have to push the Russians back all because of you, your betrayal!" It was at this moment that Epitaph just calmly reached inside Hitler's jacket and took hold of the Walther PPK Seven Point Sixty-Five Millimeter Pistol that was always there. "Don't worry, you'll still go down as a hero." Epitaph told Hitler before he put the semi-automatic pistol to the dictators temple and pulled the trigger. Eva didn't have a chance to scream before the guards that held her snapped her neck. Of course Epitaph and his men were gone long before Hitler's guards got in and found the dead dictator.

Well you can probably guess by now who Epitaph sent out to handle the Russians. Yep, that would be I. Once again we were disguised as Nazi troops, blending right in with them. So much so that they never thought anything strange about us.

Minor operations did continue in the west and on May eighth, nineteen forty-five England finally surrendered to Nazi Germany. This effectively confined The United States to their own continent and for the next few months they were the target of Nazi air raids. They were repeatedly asked to surrender but they stubbornly refused. They started to think twice about this when on August sixth Washington D.C. was hit with the worlds first nuclear bomb. They tried to relocate the capital to Philadelphia when just three days later it too was nuked to oblivion. The United States formally surrendered on September second, nineteen forty-five. The same day Nazi Germany also signed a armistice with Russia.

Now lets take a pause for the cause here and let me tell you a little something that you may or may not like. It depends on what side of the fence you stand on. If your one of those peace loving hippies your probably not going to like this. I know a lot of you twenty-first centurions are into celebrating a event that you refer to as International Pot Smokers Day or more commonly called Four-Twenty. Don't deny it, you know what I'm talking about. When you wake up at four twenty A.M. on the twentieth day of the fourth month, which is April twentieth and puff tough on a little bit of reefer. Well allow me to inform you of the origins of this event. You see, in the nineteen thirties and early forties, unbeknownst to the German population their mighty leader, the greatest Germanic hero since Hermann The German, Adolf Hitler was quite the pot head. Come on, don't look surprised, what do you think got him through the war for all those years. Very few people knew. Only those who were in his immediate circle and some high ranking military officers had any idea. Well, after Germany won the war, starting in nineteen forty-six those who knew of Hitler's habit would get together on his birthday, April twentieth at four twenty A.M. and smoke a fatty in honor of their fallen leader. Now I don't know about you but my watch say's that right now it's four nineteen, you don't happen to have a minute to spare now do you? Go ahead, raise your bong and make a toast. It's Happy Hitler Day.

Part IX

The Western Hemisphere

Hey, what do you know, I see you did have a minute to spare. It's about time you put your head on right, after all you've had it buried in the sand this entire story.

In fourteen ninty-two Columbus sailed the ocean blue, well I don't know how the rest of it goes but anywho. No one, not even Columbus knew what he was sailing into that fateful day. Not many bought into his theory that to go east you must sail west. People were still superstitious in those times and believed the world too be flat. They also thought the ocean too be filled with sea monsters and such things, so when he never returned from his little adventure it didn't take long for people too start spreading rumors. How horrible it must have been. To be sailing along and then all of the sudden, woosh your tumbling into nothingness as if you sailed right off of a gigantic waterfall. One that would easily put Niagara to shame. And the sailors. Some of them trying desperately to grasp on to anything so that they don't enter the great void while the rest of the crew freefalls and tumbles into the dark oblivion. Oh the humanity! Those poor souls who were crazy enough to follow him on his fools errand. For decades later all sailors were afraid too be out of eyesight of land.

Had he actually reached the land of the new world he would have found a place rich with forests and rivers, mountains and valleys and yes, gold and silver. He would have also have found bronze natives that lived at one with nature.

In due time Europeans would eventually cross the Atlantic and intrude on this land. Brutally slaughtering the natives and slowly taking over. They would establish colonies that would rebel against their parent nations and The United States Of America was one of these colonies.

Almost thirty years after defeating their life-giver Britain and winning it's independence The United States, in eighteen twelve once again declared war against the island nation. The United States probably should have thought this out a little bit. From the first moments of the war the Brit's were kicking the crap out of the yanks. Smacking them around like you would a red-headed step child. This scene was played out time and time again for the next two years. In the summer of eighteen fourteen The British were moving up and down Chesapeake Bay at will, looting and plundering villages all along the coast. After that they did the unthinkable. They sacked D.C. and burned it to the ground. How much worse can it get?

Oh it's about too get worse alright, at least if your a American. Epitaph ordered me too take advantage of this situation by disguising our troops as Brits and too annihilate the Americans as if they were a anthill in the backyard that you would douse with gas, boy he really loves Americans can't you tell. If I remember correctly he is an American. Oh well. He says after this mission, which he calls Operation Repo that come tomorrow we will rule the world. The thing is I've traveled through time so often now that I know longer know which tomorrow he's talking about.

I decided to approach this with a two prong attack. One on land and the other at sea. The land troops were dispatched a few miles from their target, Baltimore, Maryland at a place called North Point in the wee hours of September twelfth. They continued to march all day long toward Baltimore with little resistance. Like anyone can stop The Epitaph Army.

I personally am sitting on one of the ships that is now sailing into the Baltimore Harbour. I have a armada of early nineteenth century British looking ships. The only real difference between these and authentic British ships is that I've beefed up the armaments. You know, more modern cannons and such. I'm sitting in the cabin sipping on my bottle of rum. No need for me to be on deck my crew has this under control. Besides this will be as easy as one, two, three. It always is.

The target for my fleet is Fort McHenry. We should have this taken care of about the same time the land forces sack Baltimore. We must be pretty close now as I can hear our artillery beginning the bombardment of their fortified position. I think I'll just sit here and have another sip of rum. So tell me, what are you going too do when you wake up tomorrow and discover that Epitaph is now your ruler. The ruler of the world. It's going too be so great knowing that he is lord and master of all.

Wait a minute. What the hell was that? That didn't sound good. It sounded almost like incoming but that's impossible. Noone outside of me and my men have weapons like that in eighteen fourteen. You wait right here, I better go check this out and see whats happening.

As I stand on the deck of my flagship I can't believe what I'm looking at. Almost three quarters of my fleet is ablaze as they sink to the bottom of the harbour. How can this be? Hell this can't be! What the hell is happening here. Man, Epitaph is not going too be happy about this. "Man, I hate to cut this short but I gotta go!"

Coming Soon
Time Wars II: Rise Of A.O.T.H